AVENGED

L.V. Lane

Copyright © 2021 L.V. Lane

All rights reserved.

ISBN: 9798836968779

This is a work of fiction. Names, characters, businesses, places, events and incidents are either the products of the author's imagination or used in a fictitious manner. Any resemblance to actual persons, living or dead, or actual events is purely coincidental.

All rights reserved. This book or parts thereof may not be reproduced in any form, stored in any retrieval system, or transmitted in any form by any means—electronic, mechanical, photocopy, recording, or otherwise—without prior written permission of the author.

CONTENTS

Chapter One	Pg 1
Chapter Two	Pg 9
Chapter Three	Pg 27
Chapter Four	Pg 37
Chapter Five	Pg 51
Chapter Six	Pg 65
Chapter Seven	Pg 79
Chapter Eight	Pg 87
Chapter Nine	Pg 95
Chapter Ten	Pg 114
Chapter Eleven	Pg 123
Chapter Twelve	Pg 142
Chapter Thirteen	Pg 150
Chapter Fourteen	Pg 158
Chapter Fifteen	Pg 171
Chapter Sixteen	Pg 176
Chapter Seventeen	Pg 184
Chapter Eighteen	Pg 193

Avenged

Chapter Nineteen	Pg 201
Chapter twenty	Pg 207
Epilogue	Pg 218
About the Author	Pg 226

CHAPTER ONE

Erin

I never aspired to become a space pirate. It was more an occupation I stumbled upon while trying to survive. I grew up in a sprawling shantytown on the outskirts of Primus, just one of many orphans running the filthy streets, stealing and even begging when I could spot the right candidate, or going hungry the rest of the time. That was until Mike, a rough spaceship captain, became the wrong pocket to pick. He gave my ass a sound thrashing and took me back to his ship to work off my debt.

No one interfered. I was a leech. The people of my shantytown were glad to see me go.

I was still a kid at the time, whereas Mike was about a hundred, with more rolls of purple skin than I was comfortable getting up close and personal with. Thankfully, it turned out that Mike was a softhearted sort of brute, and the worst he did was set me to scrubbing every corner of his filthy ship. His crew, all hulking aliens of one breed or another, treated me like an overindulged brat under their feet, chuckling at my antics, which were many and inventive, and putting me to scrubbing duties on those occasions when my mischief went too far.

No one would write a sonnet about my life, but after my fateful meeting with Mike, I never went to bed hungry again.

And that was how I became a space pirate.

Until two weeks ago, when my mostly peaceful journey into space piracy came off the rails.

Today, as I finish a hard day salvaging in the ship engine room, hot and sweaty, I think about crawling straight into my bed. My tiny quarters are next to the engine room, along a narrow corridor and down a hatch out of everyone's way. The room used to be for long forgotten storage, but Mike's crew repurposed it for me. A legacy of my early life on the streets is that I don't do open spaces…or other beings. Beings and people equal danger, and space equals exposure and lack of safety—to me, they are pretty much one and the same. Mike ordered his team to rip out the supplies that had been stowed there and install a bed, portable cleansing unit, and a cupboard. Then I was good to go.

There is barely enough room for me, which is just the way I like it. With a twenty-alien strong crew and the Krinch—an essential inclusion if you don't want a riot to break out—space is a premium.

Now my room is my hideaway. The giant horned bastards who destroyed my rosy foray into space piracy can't get through the narrow hatch. It means sleep is done safely, although they expect their pound of flesh paid via my servitude if I want to see food in my belly. Space rations have always held a peculiar allure for me, but that's what happens when you grow up in a slum, going hungry half the time.

I think about going hungry now.

I think about staying down here, curling up in my bed, and letting the creeping death of hunger come for me.

Only I'm a human, and survival is hardwired into us. So instead of going to bed, I head for the canteen, where I can grab some food before I sleep and repeat the cycle of another day salvaging for the horned bastards who destroyed my dream.

You see, just as Mike turned out to be the wrong pocket to pick for me, so the Burning Titan proved to be the wrong booty to steal for Mike.

As I enter the ship canteen today, our resident Krinch is getting fucked by a horned bastard on the end booth table.

Two weeks ago, I was sitting in the same booth, playing cards with Mike and his boys and feeling happy with my lot. Mike is dead now. The horned bastards splattered his purple blood all over the metal floor and walls of the canteen within minutes of the breach.

Which is when I discovered that Mike wasn't a pirate at all, more of an opportunistic scavenger.

These are real pirates. Not the *rough around the edges, soft in the center* kind of pirate wannabes, but *mean to the core, slit your throat if you're not useful* kind of pirates. Some of Mike's crew put up a fight, not that it did them any good. All too quickly, the remainder of us were assimilated into their operation.

Our ship is no longer our ship but their ship, tacked on to the side of a much larger vessel while they strip it of anything of worth. To add further insult, the surviving crew and I are helping them in this task.

Gone is the playful banter, at least on our part. The pirates, the real ones, spend a great deal of time happy.

As I survey the crowded canteen, I regret not going straight to bed, despite the hunger gnawing at my belly.

Head low, hood pulled forward, breather mask in place

over my face, and eyes hidden behind welding goggles two sizes too big, I take advantage of the distraction to sneak through to the back, where the packaged food is kept. Half a dozen of the pirate's brethren watches the Krinch, grunting their appreciation when she emits a particularly enthusiastic scream.

It might be from pleasure, or it might be from pain. I'm not much of an expert on the nuances of fucking. Being a tagalong to a wannabe space pirate crew is not conducive to sexual exploration.

Maybe I should feel sorrier for the Krinch. Still, she's been servicing Mike and his crew for years, and anyone who could fuck a creature with slimy purple skin isn't going to be worried about a few rough pirates.

Also, Krinch are genetically engineered for sexual servitude. She has two mouths and three pussies and can only ingest semen. Basically, she's dead if she isn't fucked enough.

I've spent too much of my life hungry to feel sorry for a female who's being fed.

Today, I'm hungry enough to chew on cables. Long hours ripping components from the cramped ship underbelly, because I'm the only person who can fit, is coupled with snatching no more than a few hours' sleep a night, because I'm terrified, are taking their toll. If I don't eat some food and rest soon, I'm going to make a mistake.

No one pays attention as I shove a package into the food-bator. If it were edible raw, I'd have already taken it and fled. I mutter a curse when the touchpad doesn't respond to my gloved finger. The only reason I've flown under the radar so far is because every inch of me is covered. A few of Mike's former crew let it be known that I'm an obscure, highly poisonous lifeform useful for getting into the awkward spaces on the ship.

The horned stripy bastard, who appears to command the pirate horde, gave me a dubious look on hearing this news and set me to immediate work.

A swift glance over my shoulder, and I ascertain that everyone is still occupied. Most of them have given me a wide berth since the 'poisonous' declaration, but it pays to be cautious. Humans are unique in the galaxy, and I'm confident if anyone caught a glimpse of my flesh, it will herald the beginning of my demise.

Mike's crew were sneaking me rations, but I've not seen any of them in days. Hence, I'm so hungry. Which is why I'm taking this risk.

After a deep breath, I whip the glove off, stab the buttons for cook, and shove the glove back on.

My heart is racing a galactic mile a minute, but all I hear is the raucous encouragement, "Plug another hole!"

I'm fine. I force my breathing to slow. Just a few minutes, and I can take my prize and get out of here, back to my hideaway, where the horned fuckers can't reach me, then I can eat and catch a few hours of much needed sleep.

I'm exhausted, dirty, and my stomach feels like someone has cut a hole in it. My life has come full circle. Once a Prius brat, always a Prius brat, scavenging for my next meal before finding a place to hide.

The timer ticks down from two minutes, the bare minimum needed so I won't make myself ill. The crowd around the Krinch turns rowdier, and my tension lifts in tandem.

Thirty seconds.

The Krinch emits a high, keening wail, and my nerves stretch tight.

Twenty seconds. I can manage another twenty seconds.

A cheer goes up behind me, but I keep my eyes on the prize. Think small, be small. They believe I'm poisonous, thanks to quick thinking from Mike's former crew. I fucking love the ugly, purple-skinned wannabe pirates who took me in for the last five years.

Ten seconds.

I sense a presence behind me.

A single hand closes over mine where it rests on the counter. The horned bastards come in a variety of colors—red, black, gray, white, solid color, or with darker tips.

The clawed hand that covers mine is pure black, but

from the wrist, it's snow white where it disappears under his plated armor. I've never looked too closely at any of the horned ones until now, but frozen by my fear, my mind sucks in every horror drenched detail. Retractable claws spring to clatter against the counter. The skin isn't skin at all, but super short fur.

The hand is so big, that it swallows my gloved one with ease.

His deep voice rumbles a declaration of my doom next to my ear.

"You made a mistake, human."

CHAPTER TWO

Kane

A Krinch is getting fucked in all her many holes when I enter the canteen of our latest acquisition.

This is quite an undertaking, and I'm distracted for several seconds as I try to work out what is what among the writhing mass of limbs, bodies, and cocks.

Krinch are better suited to the three cocked Tridons, but the team is taking on the challenge.

I wince as a particularly enthusiastic thrust batters the Krinch's head into the wall.

She does not appear troubled. Then again, the species has an incredible tolerance for pain.

I do a double take at seeing the tiny poisonous one getting rations. This is the first time I've seen it since we boarded this vessel.

Edicus wanted to blast its body into space when he learned of its poisonous nature. Still, I figured it has lived among the purple folded ones for many years without apparent incident. It is tiny and so helpful in much of the necessary ship stripping. Also, if it dies, we will not be troubled in the way we would for other, more robust captives.

The Krinch chooses this moment to climax. I wince again as the high-pitched sound assaults my ears.

Then do my second double take as the poisonous one pops its ration into the food-bator. It pauses in a way I find odd before swiftly removing its glove and tapping upon the control screen.

I blink. Initially, I'm concerned about crew safety, thinking its touch left toxins. Then I'm concerned for an entirely different reason.

Only one creature in the known universe has such delicate skin in shades of white or brown—*human*. Something akin to panic whites out my mind. It is delicate, which means it's a *female*, I'm sure of this. If it—no, she is discovered, it will be chaos. Human females are the source of the sweetest sexual pleasure. There will be a riot, and its tiny, frail body will be rutted to death. Should sanity prevail, Edicus will claim her, and then he will fuck her to death.

I've whiled away many drunken nights listening to Lan's stories of mating women. I initially presumed this to be an exaggeration, since the human half-breed is prone to wild tales when inebriated. He's entertaining, and his stories often draw a crowd. Still, he spoke of fucking a human female in detail until realizing my enrapt interest, then he downplayed their allure.

Which leads me to the conclusion that he was, in fact, telling the truth.

I need to get her to safety.

As I assess the tiny, probably non-poisonous one, I realize my thoughts are not entirely virtuous in nature. I'm a pirate, so I'm relieved by this. The strange, protective emotion I first felt was a sure road to my personal ruin. What I want is to take the tiny one to my quarters, strip *it* to check if *it* is verifiably a *she*, and further, has the little petals Lan spoke so highly of, which provide a source of untold pleasure.

The need to unwrap it and inspect the tiny petals becomes an imperative. I will beat Lan bloody if his tales were an exaggeration. Well, I will try. The half-breed has skin tougher than a mystical Earth elephant, and in our many sparring sessions, my claws barely make a dent.

I move to crowd it—yet to be verified as a she—against the counter. It gasps, and even to my untrained ears, I'm convinced it is female. I fear that I will imminently be rutting *her* with all the savagery I possess. Scent washes over me, ripe and unclean, but my cocks stir regardless, straining against the hard plates of my armor until the pain brings a genuine fear I might black out.

My hand closes over her smaller, glove-clad one.

"You made a mistake, human," I say, my voice rougher than usual.

She freezes. The food-bator dings to announce the program is complete. She sighs, then surprises me by snatching the container from within. "Fine, whatever, but you're going to let me eat first."

I allow her to take the food she's so possessive about back to my allocated quarters. No one pays any attention. They are likely presuming I'm about to eject her out into space as Edicus desired. The corridor is quiet, but I still check each way carefully before taking her inside my quarters.

Spinning, she presses a gloved hand to my chest as the door clicks shut. "I eat first."

The mask muffles her voice, but it has a pleasing tone. I nod, trying not to appear too eager for her to remove the mask, yet I'm incredibly eager regardless.

A short impasse follows. I make no move to inspect her, much as I strongly want to, and she makes no move to eat.

"You eat first," I confirm, hoping to progress the situation, then gesture to my seat and table that flip down.

With a nod, she sits. The hood remains up, but she slips the mask and welding goggles off as she turns toward the food.

The hood hides most of her face, but I catch a glimpse of a small pink nose as she rips the top from the food package and begins to shovel the contents into her mouth.

I always imagined that human females would be graceful, but she is not. I've seen hardened space pirates with more grace than this tiny being.

Is the poor creature starving? I could eat once a week and be satisfied, but I remember that Lan needs to eat several times a day. She is mine now, though she's dirty and disheveled, and even if she does not have the elusive petals, I will ensure she is fed.

I try not to crowd her as she eats, but nevertheless, I am almost touching her by the time she's done.

Pushing the empty carton aside, she sends a furtive glance my way and then stills. "What are you going to do with me?" she asks.

With the mask gone, her voice is unmistakably feminine.

"Are you human?" I ask, needing her to admit as much.

I can't see her eyes, but I have an enticing view of her pretty pink lips.

"No," she says. "I'm a really obscure type of being that looks a lot like a human but is super poisonous."

Her voice is unsteady, reminding me that she is small and prey, while I am a large predator.

Also, I'm now convinced beyond doubt that she is human.

When I don't answer, her head lowers before she asks once more, "What will you do with me?"

"Keep you," I say, knowing I'll be in serious trouble should anyone find me hiding a human, yet I'm determined to do precisely that. "Inspect you," I add, although I'm thinking more about the fucking that will follow after the inspection. "And discipline you severely if you lie to me again," I finish.

In Lan's many rambling tales of human females, he emphasized their cunning nature and wiles that can cause males of any species to forget all common sense unless the female is trained and disciplined.

She nods. Her pink lips tremble, but it's for the best that she understands her situation.

"You are dependent upon me now." Why does voicing this fill me with a sense of power over her? I'm a pirate. She is a captive. I've always held power, yet keeping her here with me heightens this dynamic. "I will train you to please me. If you please me, I will care for you. If you don't, I will be forced to discipline you. You would do well to remember this."

She nods again. "Okay… Can I clean up first?"

I cannot yet see her eyes, but her plump lips are utterly captivating. She is ripe, though, and while I'm not displeased with her suggestion that she clean, I'm a little surprised. "You may." I tap the door plate on the cleansing cubical, and it pops open with a hiss. "Do not attempt to close the door."

"But won't everything get wet?"

"Do not close the fucking door and do not question me again."

Her sigh is heavy with attitude. I will have to question Lan further on the handling of human females. Although she is shaking as she gains her feet, she is not close to being mastered.

Turning her back on me, she pulls the zip down her jacket, and I forget to breathe. Next, the hood is drawn back, revealing a shock of shaggy hair in shades of brown, red, and blonde that must have been cropped with a blade. The jacket slides off, leaving only a threadbare undershirt. I take in her slim back, shoulders, and delicate neck.

My claws spring out, and my stomach muscles clench. She's *so delicate*.

She throws a look over her shoulder, and I might have

growled, but then I see the color of her eyes before she glances away.

Big, bright, electric blue.

Lan's are a glassy mud brown. I was not expecting them to come in different shades.

My stomach clenches again, and I grimace as certain parts of my body pinch against my armor plates when they predictably rise.

The jacket is folded and placed neatly beside the cleanser door. Her boots come off next. There is a pause before the undershirt is drawn over her head to reveal pale skin crisscrossed in a network of white scars.

The sight enrages me. I want to storm from the room and cut down every one of the purple folded bastards on the ship. Then reason returns. These are old scars, certainly from many weeks, months, or even years ago.

"Who did this?" I ask. My voice is rough, and I must fight to keep my claws retracted as I draw my fingertip across her skin. She is so fragile, my claws could rip through her skin, and a new scar would join the rest.

"Lots of people," she says quietly. "They're from when I was a child."

A scar on her shoulder has left a ridge, and she shivers as I trace over the curve. *Delicate, breakable, and mine.*

I step back abruptly. Hands shaking, she undoes the

buckle on her trousers, and they slide over her hips…revealing a round ass that stirs another growl from me. Another glance back, another flash of those bright eyes, and she darts into the cleanser. My booted foot hits the doorstep plate before she can snap it shut, and with a defiant glare, she hits the power button.

Water bursts from a hundred micro-jets. My body blocks much of the deluge, but it still sluices down my body armor and pools out into my room.

With her back to me, she washes.

I am getting soaked, and my room is getting soaked. There is a genuine danger that this will trigger an alarm, but I don't care about any of those problems as I watch her hands glide over her water slicked hair and body.

It cannot be more than two minutes before an alarm blares. I'm grateful that she is prompt enough to have soaped and rinsed her short hair. Her body isn't thoroughly washed, but it is washed enough, and I thump the power button and wrest her dripping body from the cubical.

I hit the override on the alarm panel, lest some interfering fucker decides to check. She is shivering, my claws have sprung out, and a thin trickle of blood oozes where they have punctured her delicate skin. I retract them.

I don't lose command of myself like this.

She's holding herself away, face averted, and I want to demand she face me. She's a captive and has no privilege beyond those I choose to give her. The need to inspect that which is now mine is compelling, and I toss her slippery form down upon the bed.

I pry her legs apart. She squeals and tries to snap them together again.

At first, all is hidden, and I'm convinced Lan has lied, but as I force her legs farther apart, the slim slit opens to reveal a treasure in between. "I won't allow my claws to cut you again," I say, staring at the petals I've exposed between her open thighs. "No matter how pleasurable you feel."

Her skin is like the softest silk under my fingers, damp from the shower, and no longer smells an unpleasant kind of ripe. I want to pad at her with my claws, even knowing it will hurt her.

I wedge my body further between her thighs. I'm soaked too. Removing my armor and drying would be advisable, but without the barrier of clothing, I fear I will fall upon the tiny non-poisonous being who I have verified is human and female.

The little nubbin Lan spoke so highly of still eludes me, but inside the outer petals are more petals, and I believe it must be hidden there. Underneath is the opening to her pussy.

"Oh please, what are you doing?" Her voice is high and anxious. She doesn't like me inspecting her. Her tiny body wriggles, testing my hold, and her pussy entrance now glistens in a way that I do not think is water.

Is she aroused?

Our females do not produce slick of any kind. It is the male who produces lubricant so that we can mate without discomfort. Yet I am convinced this is a sign of her readiness for mating. I growl, and she twitches, the tiny entrance pulsing out more slick.

She tries to cover herself with her hands, but I gather them and hold them against her stomach. My claws itch to spring out, but I temper the urge and touch her wet core with the pad of my finger.

She gasps, and her wriggling makes her clench again.

Gathering the leaking stickiness, I rub it between my fingers and thumb. It's a form of natural lubricant. I lift my fingers to my lips. My eyes roll back, and I groan, sucking my finger into my mouth. She is delicious, and I need to feast.

But first, I need to find the little nubbin.

Going back to her pussy, I part the inner folds, expecting to find it here.

Nothing? "Where is it?"

"Where is what?" Her voice has a rough edge, like she is being strangled. She has retrieved her hands while I have been distracted and now has one arm flung over her eyes as if to hide from what is happening.

"Where is your pleasure nubbin, human?" I demand.

"Nubbin?" she mutters and tries to close her legs—a pointless exercise, since I am on my knees wedged between them. If Lan lied about the nubbin, I will beat the bastard bloody. Not ready to admit defeat yet, I gather her weeping slick and work it into her inner petals.

She jolts like she has just received an electric shock.

I grin. "You are hiding it."

"Mnnn! No!"

She squirms and gasps and tries to interfere. I'm forced to pin her still again so I can continue. I'm torn between watching her face as it screws up with pleasure and the slick coated treasure between her parted legs. My fingertips are rough and not very sensitive, but she is becoming swollen and slippery under my attention, so I'm convinced the little nubbin will soon be forced to bud.

The need to taste her becomes an imperative as she fidgets and gasps. Lowering my head, I lick her nectar from the source. Sweet heaven, she is delicious. Even if the mysterious nubbin does not reveal, I am much enamored with her. I lick my tongue around her hole before plunging it inside. She arches on the bed, forcing me to pin her more securely so I can enjoy my feast.

My tongue is long and agile. The forked tips can work independently, allowing me to thoroughly explore her little cavern, which is leaking lubricant. Muttered curses begin to pour from her mouth.

I decide to explore the little petal that gave her the jolt.

She squeals and clutches at the bedding like she is holding on for dear life. It is then that I feel the nub swelling under my tongue. She gasps and moans as I work it relentlessly. My dicks spit out lubrication in anticipation, although this sweet writhing human is copious and has no need for it.

The bud is growing, and I'm so excited by this that I fear I will either ejaculate inside my armor or die of pain as the tight plates buckle under the strain. Finally, the little nubbin pokes up enough for me to wrap one fork of my tongue around it and set a gentle tugging rhythm, which I hope will encourage it to further bloom.

Her breathing becomes erratic, the thrashing turns wild, and then she screams and her small hands grasp my horns like she might wrest me off.

I lift my head, plucking her small hands away. Her body is heaving like she has engaged in strenuous exercise rather than lying on a bed. A pink flush covers her cheeks, chest, and upper breasts, and I notice her nipples have become hard and stiff.

I cup her tits, as Lan called them, which are barely enough to fill my large hands…but squeezing the rosy tips produces the same alluring jolt in the tiny human.

Interesting.

Her bright eyes flash to meet mine. She is still breathing heavily but is cognizant again.

Forced to leave her side briefly, I stow my weapons and unclip my armor down the middle. It gives my throbbing cocks some relief as I crawl up the bed over her and begin a new feast on her pretty tits.

Erin

The black and white horned bastard who has captured me goes by the name of Kane. At least that's what I call him. They have their own language, which comes out more like grunts, but my human mouth can't replicate it.

"Okay…can I get clean first?" Really, did I just say that? How fucking stupid. I must have some weird idea about meeting my end clean and with a full belly.

I've lived on the street of Primus, so I'm tough and I know how to look after myself against other humans, no matter how big. But this giant freaking badass black and white alien, in his crazy plate armor littered with guns and fuck knows what else, is terrifying me.

Only he's not terrifying me in the way I thought he would.

Two weeks ago, they killed Mike. Not this one specifically. It was the stripy bastard, Edicus, who put a blaster to the side of Mike's head, but they're all from the same demon brood and I hold them equally to blame. Then again, as I was about to get into his shower, his fingers skimming down my back as he traced a scar were gentle.

He's not gentle anymore.

My arm stings where his claws have raked me, but I didn't have a chance to worry about that because he tossed me to the bed and pried my legs open.

What the fuck is he doing with his tongue? First, I'm pinned roughly to the bed and brought to a shuddering climax in less than a minute. Next, he turns his attention to my breasts. With one grasped in his right hand, he squeezes roughly while performing voodoo with his tongue on the other side.

I'm trying not to look at it, but I already know it's forked and the two sides move around independently.

"It's all true," he mutters under his breath before swapping sides.

I'm aroused. I can't even lie to myself about the state of my body. I'm also terrified, and everything is getting muddled up in my mind. The tugging on my nipple, the way it shoots a thread of pleasure all the way to my clit, his rough handling as he cups the other side, his huge freaking alien body covered in white fur, and a brutish alien face with freaking fangs that could shred my skin, all conspire to drive me to a near delirious level of arousal.

I realize it can get worse when he licks his way back

down my body, pries my thighs wide, and latches onto my clit, which is now so sensitive, I can barely stand it. His tongue, long and dexterous, pulls relentlessly on my clit. As is inevitable under this forced sensual onslaught, I come in a glorious heady rush.

And so begins my journey into a sexual torment that never seems to end. I am pinned, and no amount of begging and thrashing will allow me to escape. Yet another climax tears me apart. I am certain my mortal soul leaves my body with the scream that leaves my throat. Dots swim before my eyes, and a hot flood of pleasure sweeps over my entire body.

I'm both deaf and blind, nothing but a bundle of over stimulated nerves and confused emotions, and throbbing everywhere.

Kane

I'm worried something is wrong, but I can't seem to stop. She whimpers and pales. I can't tell if this is a healthy sign.

My eyes lower once again to her slick pussy, which, as Lan foretold, has bewitched me. I moan as I part the little folds so I can better inspect her nubbin, now plump and swollen under the attention of my tongue. I pet it gently with my thumb as I inspect the lower parts of her pussy.

There are two little holes. I nearly fucking come. The larger one glistens invitingly, but farther down is a second smaller hole that does not appear to self-lubricate. Then I remember that humans only have one cock and my enthusiasm fades.

Still, I have often found that where there is a will, there is a way. I thrust a finger inside, and the tiny human nearly shoots off the bed.

"Oh my god! What? What! No!"

"I don't think they will both fit in the first hole," I say reasonably. "But if that is your preference, I am willing to try."

She gasps and squirms. I pin her more firmly to the bed so I can better explore the second hole that is clenching over my thrusting finger in the most arresting way.

"Good pet," I say encouragingly. "Clench around my finger. Do you need to come?"

"I—Oh! Fuck! Please!"

Her bucking body suggests she is trying to dislodge me, even as she verbally commands me to fuck. Lan did not speak about this apparent conflict. I'm not sure if I should discipline her for her forwardness in issuing a command or let the matter pass this time, given she has come so sweetly and frequently for me. Further, my cocks have reached a maddening state of arousal after I have feasted on her cunt, and I can be forgiven for not thinking straight. Lan also mentioned feminine lubricant having an aphrodisiac upon certain aliens, which is true for me.

She jolts as I squeeze a second finger in.

I can see why she does not need to self-lubricate the second hole. There is more than enough trickling from the upper one to aid the passage of my fingers. Still, she is exceptionally tight, and it is for the best that both my cocks are leaking with the same enthusiasm my cleansing cubical leaked all over my quarter's floor.

I am captivated by her breathy grasps, pointless writhing, and enthralled by the muttered begging pouring from her plump pink lips. The more I look at the lips upon her face as she twitches, the more I become convinced that her small, blunt teeth would be no impediment to a cock. Hooking my fingers deep in her second hole, thumb smashed down over her fat pleasure nubbin, I thrust two fingers of my other hand into her mouth to explore how much space there is.

"Uhhhhhh!!"

She comes. All the muscles in her little hole squeeze over my fingers in fierce clenching waves, even as she sucks deeply on my fingers in her mouth.

There is no blood left anywhere on my body. It has flooded both my dicks to such an extent, I feel a little dizzy.

I need to get my fucking armor off before I pass out.

CHAPTER THREE

Kane

The incessant beeping of an alarm somewhere in my room rips my attention from the twitching human on the bed. I bolt upright, removing my hands from the various parts of her. It takes me several valuable seconds to work out where the fuck I am.

My room.

With my human captive.

It's only now that I belatedly remember I was due for a shift when I stopped by the canteen. Fuck! Edicus does not appreciate his minions slacking off. There will be hell to pay.

"I need to go," I say. The tiny human appears adorably confused and well pleasured by me. I feel my chest puff with pride that I have done this to her. Humans are every bit as addictive as Lan indicated they were.

"Go?" She looks down and pats herself in the manner of one checking all their parts are still present and accounted for.

"Yes, go," I say, worried that she is dim-witted. "I am due for my shift."

"I was supposed to be sleeping," she says, now looking everywhere but me.

"That is good," I say, cleaning up before wrestling to close my armor up. Both cocks are fucking hard, and the pain is excruciating. Still, it will help the fucking things to go down. "You will stay here while I work." I snag my communicator and type out a message to say that I'm on my way. "Do not give me trouble." I pin her with a look, mindful of Lan's insistence that human females need to be disciplined regularly. By his account, they can cause no end of trouble if not properly controlled, and having met mine, I can well believe it. I have known her less than an hour, and already, I am late for a shift.

Mine. I like the ring to that word. The little voice in my head is cautioning me that I can't claim anyone, nor can I hope to retain possession. I am a space pirate. I live with space pirates. It is not a lifestyle conducive to mates and breeding.

I curse when my wayward thoughts send blood pounding into my cocks.

"I won't cause trouble," she says.

I don't believe a word that comes from her pretty lips. I believe that she will cause me a great deal of trouble, whether she intends to or not. "I will need to lock you in."

She blinks a few times. "They will expect me to work again soon."

"Do not question my decision, human," I say more confidently than I feel. "I will tell them you caused trouble and I ejected you from the airlock for the safety of the crew." My plan grows confusingly more elaborate under pressure. I cannot bear the thought of her leaving and wandering unattended where anyone might find her and discover she is a human and female and addictive. My claim on her is weak. Lan will try to claim her, being the closest to her kind, and if he does not, then Edicus almost certainly will. He might claim her anyway, especially if he tastes her.

My claws spring out. The tiny human eyes them warily and begins to shake.

"I will lock you in. You will stay here. I will bring food when I return." I need to fucking leave before I start inspecting her again. Pivoting, I stride from the room, hitting the lock as I exit.

She has bewitched me. Had I stayed there a moment longer, I would have inspected her and likely mounted her. Then Edicus would eject me from the airlock and claim the human for himself.... Either that, or no one would realize she was trapped and she might starve to death.

This thought troubles me greatly. By the time I arrive at the cargo docks of our recently commandeered vessel, I am very fucking tense. Opening the dock door, I walk directly into Lan, all nine feet of him, complete with a hide impenetrable by anything short of a blaster. He is not the only one. The whole fucking ship crew is present and crowded into the docking bay, forming a wall of bodies inside the door.

"Sorry," Lan rumbles, glancing down at me, even as he grasps my arms like he is worried I will topple over, which is a fucking insult, given I am a Devlin warrior and arguably the most lethal being in the universe.

"What the fuck are you doing behind the door?" I mutter.

"You're late," he says, thumbing toward Edicus, who paces in front of the purple-skinned pirate failures who fucked over one of our supply runs last month. "I was covering for you. When Edicus asked where you were, I said you were behind me."

I raise a brow before eyeing the proceedings ahead. "And he believed you?"

"I don't think he did. But he was distracted by the purple-skinned ones who tried to poison his air in his sleep."

"Ah," I say, nodding slowly. "That is a sure way to piss him off. What's happening now?"

"He's about to eject them out the airlock, I believe," Lan says, jerking his head toward where the purple bastards are all lined up, looking more purple in the face of their imminent death. "We've lost the poisonous one. That's the only thing holding up the proceedings. None of them will say where it is. Edicus is determined to beat and torture them all to death if they don't offer up its whereabouts. For all they are slimy bastards who ripped our ship off, they are loyal. He's already killed two, and no hints of a confession yet."

Fuck! Thank fuck I locked her in the room! Edicus would likely blast her into space, whether she was a human female or not. He is unstable at the best of times, but a poisoning attempt is likely to make him particularly uncivilized.

"We'll have to strip ship ourselves now," Lan continues, like I am not having a small mental breakdown.

"I need you to cover for me," I say, sidling up closer to him.

"Cover?" He fixes mud brown eyes on me. They narrow.

"What the fuck have you done?"

There is no easy way to confess this. I have captured a human, one that does not even rightfully belong to me. I'm not the commander of our pirate brigade, merely a crew member. A purple-skinned failed pirate screams as Edicus begins his torture. I sigh heavily. "I took the poisonous one to my room."

"What the fuck, Kane. Why would you do something like that?"

"Hush!" I hiss back at him, whipping him with my tail. Everyone nearby is glaring at us. "I saw its—her hands when she went into the food-bater. "

"Fuck! Was it trying to infect the ship?" He nods his head toward the now silent purple-skinned one who is being tossed into the airlock portal. Edicus hits the button to eject it into space before focusing on the next in the long line. "Wait! You just said *her*."

I roll my fucking eyes before lashing him with my tail. "Exactly," I whisper. "It is not poisonous at all, but a human and a female."

His wings, which are more often compact against him in the manner of a backpack, spring. Brick, who is standing on his left, grunts when one hits him in the face. He nearly mows me over in his enthusiasm to get to the door. I'm forced to whip him again to gain his attention.

"Ouch!" He rubs the back of his thigh while frowning

down at me.

"It barely touched you," I say, throwing a swift glance toward Edicus, who is torturing the next purple-skinned one and thankfully not paying attention to us. "Yes, *it* is a *she*—a human she. I realized what she was and stowed her in my quarters to thoroughly inspected her. She is both addictive and tricky. I have yet to discipline her, but I'm already suspecting she will cause me trouble."

"Fuck! Edicus will toss you out the airlock and keep it—her for himself if he finds out. Are you sure it is human and female? Perhaps I should inspect her similarly, given I am the only one of us qualified for this task."

"I am very fucking sure. It was exactly as you described a human female, complete with the pleasure nubbin, which it tried to hide."

"She," he mutters a little wistfully now.

"She," I agree. I have spent a lot of time thinking of it and now need to adjust, given I have verified it as a woman. "I locked her in my room. I cannot let her go about the ship now, and especially given Edicus is on the warpath. He might kill her anyway or claim her for himself."

"You claimed her then?" Lan asks as another purple pirate gets jettisoned out of the airlock. The line is diminishing. Soon, Edicus will turn his attention elsewhere.

"I have not claimed her," I say, wishing I hadn't mentioned my pet at all. "Yet. I got a message about being late and was forced to leave her before I could complete the claim."

"That's a bit of a risk," Lan says, face turning grave. "What if someone else goes in your quarters? What's her name anyway?"

"Why would anyone go in my quarters?" I mutter, although I am now wondering about her name.

"You don't know her name, do you?" he asks smugly, pointing toward my crotch and copping a funny look from Brick, who is standing to Lan's left. "Too busy thinking with your two cocks. She might reject your claim, given you haven't even asked her name."

"She can't reject my claim." Only I don't sound very confident about this. Can she reject my claim? Is there a loophole in the claim of a human female that Lan has failed to tell me about? "I need to go back to the room."

"You can't," he says, stone-colored face lifting with amusement at my expense. "It's your shift. As you said, you will need someone to cover for you," he continues. "An ally. Managing a woman is a two-being job. You already admitted as much. I want rights to woo the human for claiming. It is only fair."

"I will skewer your thick hide if you—"

"You can try." He grins. "Unlike you, my shift is over now. Yours has just begun."

My claws spring out. I am about to maim the fucker.

"Kane, Lan!" Edicus' roar cuts through our verbal sparring, which was in danger of shifting toward a physical altercation.

Both our heads swing his way.

"Organize a ship search for the poisonous one!"

It is only now that I realize the purple pirate failures have disappeared, blasted into deep space, I presume. "It has gone," I say. "I caught it attempting to infect the kitchen, and I ejected it into space."

Edicus' stripy gray face turns a deeper shade of gray.

"You've really fucked up now," Lan mutters beside me.

Edicus points at the airlock and glowers like he's thinking of tossing me after them. "Were you still fucking asleep? Did you not see me beating the purple-skinned fuckers to find out where *it* was?"

"I thought you were merely having sport with them," I say, a little defensively. This is a fair comment. Edicus has been known to have sport with beings of all kinds, asking questions that have no answer.

He stares at me, jaw locked tight and nostrils flared, while his tail lashes from side to side in a show of aggression. I hold my ground, since showing weakness before Edicus is a sure road to ruin.

Suddenly, he relaxes and his face splits in a grin. "I never trusted the sneaky little fucker. I'm relieved it has gone." He now turns to the wider pirate group. "Get back to work. We are two days from Helli Sull, and I want the ship stripped and ready for salvage in time."

The pirates disperse.

"Tell me your code," Lan says, shadowing me as I turn around.

Edicus is still watching us. I know he suspects something. I am torn. Guarding such prime and coveted breeding stock from the threat of other mates is an imperative, but so is keeping her safe.

Her safety wins out, and reluctantly, I tell Lan my door code. He walks off whistling, the bastard, while I go to begin my shift.

CHAPTER FOUR

Erin

After Kane exits the room, I lie on the bed for several long seconds in abject shock. My body is throbbing. I can't remember how many times I just climaxed. Kane seemed obsessed with inspecting me.

Fuck! I'm here in a fucking pirate's room. He put me here and told me he was claiming me before locking me in and leaving. I'm off the bed with greater haste than my pleasure racked body appreciates, grasping damp hair in my fists as I pace about. I'm the cleanest I've been in days, which is a small bonus. But what the fuck am I supposed to do? Where am I going to go?

I could hide in my room. I overheard earlier about us docking in two days. Although they might rip the ship apart to reach me. The hatch is small, but they could get in if they had a mind to. Still, how would they know I was there? Can I get over there without anybody spotting me? What about when I don't show up for work later?

I wonder how long I've been here, an hour or two, I'd guess. I don't usually take more than two or three hours for rest before someone is hollering for me.

I need to get dressed.

My hands shake as I retrieve my clothes and fumble to put them on. My ass aches. I can't believe Kane shoved his fingers into it. What if he'd sprung those lethal freaking claws? I can't believe I came while he was doing it. What the fuck is wrong with me?

I pull my pants on, throw my threadbare top over my head, shove my feet in my boots, and pull the straps tight. Next comes my jacket, goggles, and mask. Finally, I pull my hood up.

I'm a nervous wreck, which is embarrassing for a former street rat.

I take a deep breath. Time to get the fuck out of here.

True to his word, he's locked me in. That's not a

problem. I know how to pop a lock. After living on this ship for five years, I know my way around it. Before I can second-guess myself, I rip off the cover on the door panel, cut the cables, and re-wire them together to short-circuit the lock.

The door swishes open, and I step out.

The corridor is blissfully empty, but he might have notifications sent to him. I need to be long gone by then. Running will draw attention, but I still take off down the springy metal passage at an absolute sprint, round the corner, and clatter up the narrow stairs two at a time. The mesh is lightweight and bounces under my swift passage. Fuck knows how it doesn't buckle under the weight of the pirate bastards.

At the T-junction, I turn right and collide with an unexpected wall.

"Uff!" All the air leaves my lungs in a whoosh, and I land on my ass. The fall knocks my goggles askew, and my mask falls around my chin.

A mountain of a man stands before me. I use the term 'man' loosely. He looks humanoid, except he is twice the size of a human and has the stability of a wall. His entire body has the appearance of granite or stone. His ears are strange and close to his head, but also pointy. They look velvety, and I very much want to pet them. Two spike-tipped wings curve over his back, tucked close to his head. I can't tell where his armor begins and ends, as his face and hands are the same shade. Perhaps the entire thing is exoskeleton and he's a tiny blob inside?

No, his eyes are real and proportional, warm and brown. They narrow on me.

Gargoyle.

They are warring people and pretty much indestructible.

I dive straight between his legs—he's that tall. He curses, but I scramble to my feet and sprint for freedom.

He chases after me. The mesh floor creaks and groans and bounces wildly under his immense weight. Fuck me! I think his running might break the ship apart!

I'm running out of corridor, and I'm not losing him. Ahead is a sealed door leading to engineering. I slam my hand against the door plate. It pops open just as I'm plucked from my feet.

An enormous, rough hand clamps over my mouth and nose. It covers most of my face.

I can't breathe.

I can't fucking breathe!

His hands are like… I've heard the expression *hands like shovels*, but his really are!

"Keep quiet, foolish human," he says. "If they find you, they will eject you from the airlock like they did the purple-skinned pirate flunks."

I go limp.

He peels his fingers away from my face. Tears pool in my eyes as I glance over my shoulder at the stone mountain holding me. My lips quiver. I'm not an emotional person. My life saw that scoured away long ago. Yet those wannabe pirates with too many folds of purple skin were the closest thing to family I had.

"Gone?" I whisper.

He nods, face grave. "You need to hide, or Edicus will jettison you out the airlock as well. Do not give me trouble. I do not wish you to die." There is a strange honesty to this mountainous alien.

"I am Lan," he says. "And who are you, little human?"

"Erin," I say, feeling comforted by this exchange. "My name is Erin."

He nods. "I will take you back to Kane's room. It is a safe place."

"I, ah, broke the lock," I confess. Lan's hands are not on me anymore. I could make a break for it, but I find I trust him.

"Ha!" His face cracks into a grin. "Kane will be grumpy, especially when I taunt him for not keeping you properly controlled. I best take you to my room, although it will not please him."

I eye him nervously, not liking the way he said I was not

controlled. Now I'm thinking about running again, only before I can act, he plucks me from the ground, tosses me over his shoulder—avoiding his spike-tipped wing—and marches back down the corridor.

"You can't just take me," I say, although it's clear that he can. I hear voices approaching, but he turns abruptly left before hustling down the corridor, bouncing me about.

I keep my head low, worried about hitting it on the ceiling, which he skims by inches. He takes a right, then another left…and turns into an old storeroom.

Here he drops me to my feet and hits a button beside the door.

I've never been inside this old storage room before, which is now empty, save for a mattress tossed to the floor. I'm not sure what to expect, but he pushes my hood back, plucks the goggles off, and pushes my mask down until it rests around my throat, all while I stand gaping at him. Then, with surprising gentleness, he takes a lock of my hair in his enormous fingers and pets it.

When have I ever experienced gentleness in my life? This great brute, this pirate—a real pirate, not the wannabe kind—treats me as though I might break.

"Can I inspect you?" he asks.

I bat his hand away and take a step back. "You may not inspect me."

He stands up straight and promptly bangs his head on

the ceiling, wincing before leaning forward again. "This fucking ship is not built for me," he mutters as he rubs his head.

Lan is strange and endearing. That he stopped raises him to hero status in my mind, given he's a pirate.

"You are a woman then," he says, gesturing toward me with one massive hand.

"I am a woman," I agree.

"He has claimed you?"

"He has not fucking claimed me," I state vehemently. He can only be talking about Kane.

The stone giant's eyes widen. "May I woo you then? Since he hasn't claimed you."

"What? Woo?" I take another step back, but he steps forward. Given he is twice my size, it brings him close enough that my nose is inches away from his belly. Fuck! Is he…is he naked? Now I am staring at him, trying to decide if the stone is armor or a naked being who does not need to wear any. There is an indentation in the middle of his belly between what I now believe to be slabs of muscle, which looks like a belly button. No one would replicate a belly button on armor.

"Are you wearing any clothes?" I demand a little breathlessly. If he's not wearing any clothes, where the fuck is he hiding his cock?

Maybe he's not even male?

"I have pants and boots on," he says, lifting one giant foot and putting it back down with a thud that vibrates through the soles of my feet. He was right—this ship was not designed for his massive weight.

I swallow. "You are male?" I peer up into his eyes.

"I am male," he confirms. "Do you wish to inspect me?" His hand goes to his waist, where I belatedly notice a ridge indicating where his pants end and his body begins.

Waving both hands to ward him off, I step back, finding a wall behind me and nowhere else to go. "No, I do not want to inspect you." I avert my gaze. Fuck! I can't even think about what sort of cock he might have hidden in there. My eyes, of their own accord, go straight to his crotch.

"I think you do want to inspect me," he says. "Go ahead. I don't mind."

"No thank you!"

"Kane has not claimed you. Somebody needs to."

"Why does somebody need to claim me?" They are both obsessed with claiming me. I shake my head, trying to keep up with this conversation.

"If we don't claim you, Edicus will eject you out the airlock or maybe claim you for himself. It is hard to say which might be worse."

I swallow. Edicus is the stripy one. He put a blaster to

the side of Mike's head. No, I can't think about that and retain my sanity. I've seen all manner of horrors in my life—death, beatings, the kinds of things that happen to women when they don't have protection. Edicus terrifies me. I'm too young to die. "Will it keep me safe?" I ask quietly. "If I'm claimed by one of you?"

He makes a strange rumbling noise in his chest that sounds like rocks banging together. "I don't know," he says with a kind of honesty that makes my heart clench and reminds me that he is a pirate, albeit a strangely gentle one. He crouches, bringing him eye level to me. Somehow by crouching, he emphasizes how enormous he is. Only I'm not afraid, although I ought to be. He's not like Kane. He's definitely not like Edicus. He's still a pirate, I remind myself, but what does that even mean?

I've been a pirate for the last five years. At least I thought I was. Now I realize I've not been a very good one. In fact, I think my purple-skinned companions who once owned this ship, and whom I came to love, were the worst pirates in the galaxy.

"I would give my life to keep you safe," Lan says, and yet more of his honesty is reflected in his dark eyes.

Stupid tears pool behind mine. He reaches out one giant hand as though to brush them away. He stops before he touches me, fingers curling into a fist that he lowers to his side. "I won't hurt you," he says. "I've never hurt anyone unless they mess with me and mine. But I will keep you safe as best I can. If I'm honest, I'd rather inspect you and woo you, with the intention to make you my mate. I'm half human." He taps his chest. "I realize there is not much evidence of this, but rest assured, we are compatible. I have been with women before, a long time ago, when I was younger and not so large."

A slight tremble enters my hands. I cannot imagine how he could be with a woman unless he has a tiny cock. I blink a few times, forcing myself not to peek again. "And they were okay, um, after?" Why am I asking him this?

His strange stone lips tug up on one side. "They were a little…" He pauses as though searching for the word. "Tender. But well satisfied." He shrugs his big shoulders.

I swallow again. My body still throbs from what Kane did to me. I think he has broken my mind.

"Kane will not return for many hours. He asked me to take care of you, which means not letting you wander the corridors," he says, shaking his head slowly. "If Edicus or any of the others find you, I cannot say what will happen, but I don't believe it would be good."

There is no artifice in this male. He is a surprisingly genuine being. Either that, or he has amazing acting skills. Only I don't think pirates—wannabe purple-skinned ones or the real ones, which he is—care much for acting or pretenses. He is a stone mountain of a beast who could destroy me if he chose, but here he is, crouched beside me, boxing me in, yet I feel no fear.

I reach out tentatively like he did, only I don't stop until my hand presses against his buff-colored cheek. He is warm to the touch—I expected him to be cold—and a little rough, but not as rough as he appears. I find myself smiling as my hand trails down his throat until it rests against his collarbone. His skin is more like armor.

"You do not seem displeased," he says before his lips form a smile. "You realize you are inspecting me?"

I suppose I am.

"Do you want to see my cock now? Then you may decide if I'm acceptable."

"What? No!" I shake my head vigorously, although I do not take my hand back.

"You have rejected Kane. I told him as much. Don't worry about him. I do not spar him often. He is ferocious. Devlins are extremely dangerous. Unfortunately for Kane, my skin is tough. If you wish me to battle him, I will, although I consider him my friend and I would rather not."

My hand finally drops away. "I don't want you to battle him."

"Then you wish to be claimed by us both?"

"I…ah." I'm sure I don't, but the words don't make it past my tight throat. This conversation is a minefield. His big hands move to encircle my waist. They are warm and comforting through my clothing. He is powerful beyond my reckoning, yet he is gentle with me.

"I wish very much to inspect you."

I nod. "Okay," I say. I think my mind has shut down. Am I frightened? I was frightened when Kane inspected me, terrified until he dragged pleasure from me. Now I can't work out what the fuck I am.

There is no preamble. Lan strips me with methodical intent. As my threadbare top is tugged over my head, exposing my breasts, he groans. "Beautiful," he rumbles.

Only I don't feel beautiful. Beautiful is like a flower or a star cluster on the horizon. Beautiful is raindrops on the tin roofs of the shantytown where I once lived, washing the filth away.

Beautiful was once surviving to live another day.

But I, little wannabe pirate brat, am not beautiful at all.

His dark eyes glisten as he takes me in. His fingers are at the buttons on my trousers, and I hear the unmistakable sound of material tearing. He freezes and sends me a furtive look.

"Let me," I say. Lan is strangely sweet in his concern, and I would like him to inspect me if his inspecting me is anything like… No, I'm not going to think about Kane now.

I kick off my boots and shuck my trousers down.

He growls, a sound like rocks banging together.

I squeak as I find myself on my back on his giant mattress on the floor. It smells strange, clean but dusty. It sort of smells like him.

I expect him to go for something obvious, like my breasts or pussy, but he doesn't. He takes my hand within his giant one and inspects it like he has never seen a hand before. He opens all the fingers and carefully closes them again. Then he spreads them out and presses my palm to his. We look ridiculous against one another.

He grins as though caught in wonder. "So tiny and delicate. I'll be careful with you."

I believe him.

Then he presses his strange warm stone textured lips to my palm, and my breath catches in my throat. I feel the wetness as he laps against the skin. It tickles and makes me giggle…right until he stuffs my fingers into his mouth.

I squeak, thinking he is about to bite me.

He sucks while that deep rumble of stones knocking together comes from his chest. Then he pulls my fingers from his mouth with a pop, and goose bumps break out across the surface of my skin.

His face is no longer playful, but wearing an expression of intense longing that ignites a flame inside me. His giant hand encloses one breast. He squeezes gently before brushing his fat thumb across my puckered nipple.

I twitch as intense pleasure shoots all the way to my core. After Kane's earlier attention, I still buzz with arousal, and Lan dials that back up.

His eyes shift to meet mine, and the rumbling rocks smash together deep in his chest. "Beautiful," he murmurs again, leaning down and lapping at my breast with his broad, roughened tongue.

So begins my torment as he pinches, pets, and coaxes me to pleasure. As his attention turns toward my weeping pussy, I'm feverish with need.

With the first sweeping lick of his broad tongue, I know I'm already doomed.

I arch up, and he rumbles his approval.

I think I'm going to come.

I do. Three sweeping licks are all it takes, and I'm splintering and coming and gasping while the rocks knock together in his chest, louder, deeper. He laps at me enthusiastically, with big licks, his rough tongue catching everything at once. His huge hands clasp my thighs, holding me gently apart and making it clear he intends to feast. I should be terrified, yet I've never felt so safe.

My most intimate places become oversensitive under his relentless pleasuring. I try to wriggle away, but I can't. I plead, but it's like he's under a trance and keeps going back for more.

I'm going to come again. I know I am.

I do.

CHAPTER FIVE

Kane

I have spent twelve hours in mind-numbing drudgery, dragging stocks from our confiscated spaceship to our own, ready for selling when we reach the port tomorrow. When I signed up as a pirate, this wasn't what I had in mind. Maybe killing, a little blood sport, indulging in my love of violence. But the fact is that piracy is often very dull.

The matter is made worse by the fact that all I can think

about is my human captive stowed away in my room. I worry that Lan is indulging himself with what I consider mine. I realize I needed to confide in him and trust him. Lan is probably the only trustworthy bastard in the entire pirate crew. I don't even know how he got into piracy. He is a very honest sort of pirate. In fact, he's not really a pirate at all. Today, I'm glad he's around, yet also anxious to get to my room, where I can fully claim the unnamed human.

I've also spent the day avoiding Edicus, who is sure to be pissed after the incident in the docking bay. I am likewise in a bad mood being forced to do all the hard work after he ejected the purple-skinned bastards out of the fucking airlock. There is not a lot of joy or happiness all around, but the prospect of returning to my quarters, where I can thoroughly inspect my human, rouses some level of cheer.

Only the cheer does not last, for when I enter my quarters, there is no human and no Lan. The control panel inside the door has been ripped off, and the controls destroyed.

My tail swishes from side to side. Where the fuck is Lan? Where the fuck is my captive? Why the fuck didn't he message me?

Has he taken her?

I hit my communicator. He doesn't fucking answer for long, long seconds, and then he answers and sounds like he is fucking drunk. "Where the fuck are you?" I demand.

"In my room," he says, as though this is obvious when it is not obvious at all.

I growl. Further details are not required. She is with him, my human female whose name I still don't know, but I'm certain Lan, with all his gentleness, will. Not recognizing Lan as a threat was a big fucking mistake. He has often told me of his expertise at wooing human females. I thought his words were bravado, a tall tale, which he is known to do. But now…now I suspect they were not, given everything he said about them is true.

Rage building, I storm back along the corridors, ignoring everyone I pass, until I reach the storeroom, which Lan, being too big for regular cabins while we are on this commandeered ship, has claimed as his own.

I slam my palm against the entry plate, which pops open. It's not even fucking locked. She is on the bed. My tail lashes from side to side. I look between the sleeping woman and the male standing to the side. He's got his pants on, so that's something, although he looks fucking guilty. How did he ever become a pirate?

"She's naked," I point out, my voice low because…she looks adorable and I don't want to wake her up. I believe I have just lost all credibility as a space pirate. This is clearly why human females are considered both tricky and addictive.

He nods. "All tired out."

"Have you fucked her?"

"No," he says in a whisper that is closer to a thunderclap, while vigorously shaking his head. "No, I haven't."

I send the glance toward the bed, worried he will fucking wake her up. I don't want to step outside his quarters to discuss this. Edicus might see us. I've been avoiding the angry bastard all day, and I don't want to bump into him now.

"Keep your voice down."

He offers me a helpless, pained look.

Yeah, that was a low blow.

"What have you done to her?" I stab a finger in her direction.

He swipes a hand over his bald head. "Pleasured her," he says. "Although I haven't mated her yet. We agreed I could woo her."

"We agreed on nothing of the sort," I point out. We had barely started discussing what we would do when I was forced to start my shift. "You have stepped over the line."

He eyeballs my restless tail and shifts uneasily, knowing what it means. "Do not shed blood in the room while Erin is sleeping," he hisses back.

My eyes widen. So he *has* learned her name. That was also a low blow, although I cannot say I blame him. It was negligent on my part not to have asked her. In my defense,

I was distracted by her discovery on the ship and not thinking fucking straight.

"I know your weak spots," I say, just so we are clear.

"And I know how to defend them," he retorts.

The sleeping woman in the bed frets, fidgets, and finally opens her eyes. She blinks between us before clutching the blanket to her chest.

It is no use. I'm distracted. "Leave us," I say, letting my tail swish, ensuring he knows I am close to my limit. For all he thinks he can defend his weak spots, I will find them if I have a mind to.

He sighs heavily.

"It is your fucking shift," I say. "We have already drawn attention to ourselves. Do not tempt Edicus' interest further."

"Fine," he says, "But do not fucking damage her, or you and I will have words." He hits the door button and leaves the room.

Erin stares after him, still clutching the blanket. "How long will he be gone?" Her sleepy, rumpled state and nakedness is evidence of how Lan pleasured her and tried to woo her, the bastard. Now I will need to start all over again. As I reach for the buckles on my armor, she follows the movements, swallows, and glances between the door and me. "Lan has wooed you. Now it is my turn."

Her nostrils flare. "You are not very polite," she says.

"I'm a pirate," I point out. "Now, where were we?" I elect not to take the armor completely off, just loosening it enough so that my cocks don't feel like they're being strangled. The fact that he has had his hands on her pricks at my temper, but that is my own fault for trusting Lan with such an addictive being.

I crawl onto the bed, and she tries to scoot away.

I grab the blanket, but she holds it tightly to her.

I tug. She has a surprisingly fierce grip.

"Uff!"

As I rip the blanket from her grasp, she comes with it, crashing against me.

"Got you," I say. I had forgotten the allure of her naked body, now bearing a few claiming marks. My temper spikes, and my arousal follows straight afterward, seeing the distinct red patches around her breasts. "Did he hurt you?"

"No," she squeaks out as I stare, chest heaving, at the faint bruising upon her breasts. "It was... Lan was surprisingly gentle, if a little enthusiastic."

"He has marked you," I say. "You have *allowed* him to mark you."

"He was only, um, kissing me."

"He was staking his fucking claim." I have her on her back in a flash, and after gathering her small wrists in one hand, I pin them above her head. A growl rumbles in my chest as I trace my nose across the plump swell of one breast and then the other. "I'll need to mark you now too."

She doesn't dispute this, nor tell me no. I squeeze her breast in my hand and lower my head, swirling my tongue over the soft skin before closing my lips against the flesh and sucking.

She wriggles and squirms. "Please! What are you doing?"

Only she knows what I am doing, and I pin her with a look before finding a fresh place to mark.

Her lips fall open on a pant, and her eyes turn hooded as I hold her gaze and suck. I like the way she feels against me, wriggling and getting needy.

Lifting my head, I admire my blooming mark. "I'm going to need a few more." My chest rises and falls unsteadily as I sink deeper under the spell of the human I have captured. "I am not like Lan."

"I know that," she whispers. "I understand."

Good, it is for the best that she does. I will not fawn over her, although I have no desire to harm her. I recall all too well how swiftly she grew slick between her petals, as if enticing me to rut. Lips closing over her plump nipple, I suck gently. I don't believe she would appreciate it if I tried to mark her here, but I am thinking about it nevertheless. Breathy gasps and the scent of her arousal soon follows. I feast to one side and then the other, licking and lapping all over her plump tits. Her needy whimpers, wriggling, and rich aroused smell that perfumes the air, all drive me to the brink of personal destruction. I can see why humans are so coveted, why everybody wants one, and why they are highly prized.

My mind digresses to a fantasy where I claim her and keep her for myself. I get to wondering how I can make this happen, and impossible scenarios arise, one after another. I cannot continue to be a pirate, that much is certain, but it is not so easy to become something else when this is all I have known. I have a little money of my own, but is it enough?

Then there is Edicus, who does not let his people go. Plus, I'm useful to him.

If I want to claim and keep Erin, I need to find a way. I move on to her pussy, licking up her offering, getting my tongue deep inside. This time, she only makes a slight murmur when I press my finger in the smaller hole. My cocks have become painfully engorged.

I'm ready to mount her. I need to make her mine.

Erin

There is too much stimulation—his hands, tongue, and his primal desire that he must mark me. I shouldn't like this, but I do.

I have never been with anyone intimately. When I left

the shantytown, I was still a child, and I'm not exactly old now. I used to dream that Mike would bring another human into his crew and we would spend the rest of our life together as pirates. Only Mike is dead, and we weren't really pirates. Those former childlike fantasies are nothing but space dust.

I understand what comes next. Kane was interrupted last time. This time, he has just finished his shift, and Lan is gone. Yet what would or could Lan do? The strange gargoyle said he would protect me, but there is something about Kane that tells me Lan wouldn't find it easy.

Not that it matters, I've reached a point of no return. A little voice in the back of my head tells me I should bring this to a stop, but I don't listen. Only Kane has the power to sate this terrible aching need and overwrite the constant fear surrounding my life. I fall to begging, demanding, and finally, out of sheer desperation, I grasp both his horns.

Head lifting, he moans.

Are they sensitive? But no, surely he uses them in battle?

Fire heats my belly, and I scrape my nails along the length to test out my theory. He shudders, eyes glowing with ungodly need.

He surges upward, ripping the buckles of his suit apart, then shucking it down.

I stare in wonder. Kane's body is covered in white fur, all the way to his wrists and tail, where it turns black and shorter. The fur over his belly is thick and fluffy. I want to pet it. His long, powerful tail whips back and forth. Sometimes when he does it, I sense that he is annoyed, but now, it seems to represent his state of heightened arousal.

Then the bottom half of his armor drops, and I see what's nestled between his thick thighs.

I swallow, trying to work out if I've lost my mind or if he really does have two cocks. The top one points upright, while the lower one is similarly pointing up at a slight angle. They are thick, long, black, and covered with ridges and lumps.

Hysteria bubbles up in my chest as all his previous comments come rushing back… *"I don't think they will both fit in the first hole,"* he said. *"But if that is your preference, I am willing to try."*

"I don't… I—" I want to explain that I don't have two pussies. Now I understand why he was exploring my back hole. "That's not where it's supposed to go. I don't have a place for both!"

"Hush, tiny human," he says, coming down over me. He gathers my hands again and pins them above my head to the bed. "You are wet and slick. My cocks produce lubricant. Everything will fit."

I shake my head. I'm a virgin. My ass is assuredly virgin as well. I'm worried enough about my pussy taking his cock. I can't begin to think about the rest. My breathing turns choppy, and not in a good kind of way. I'm hyperventilating and verging on outright panic.

Then he's at my entrance, and I twitch. I am mentally prepared to die, yet as he sinks a little way into me, I realize that he penetrates me only with the lower cock, while the upper brushes pleasurably against my throbbing clit.

Relief that he is not going to rip my ass in two is short-lived, since he grasps my hips and slams all the way in.

I squeal.

His mouth slants over mine, forked tongue curling around mine as he kisses me silly while thrusting erratically. He did not lie about the lubricant—his cock feels wet and slippery. It doesn't matter how my body rebels against the intrusion, he slips easily in and out.

I'm full. I can't work out what is happening. It feels like Kane is everywhere. He is too big, stretching me, making me ache deep inside, but he is also pumping over and over, mesmerizing me with every thrust and retreat. I love the sensation of him moving as he finds a rhythm, the way his upper cock slides back and forth over my clit.

Everything shifts in an instant as fear and pain are overwritten by sharp pleasure. I have nothing to reconcile this moment with. An alien is fucking me with his monstrous cock.

"Good pet," he says. "You feel so hot, tight, and welcoming around my cock. It's like you are gripping me, trying to pull me back in."

I mumble, but I've no idea what I'm trying to say.

"Do you need more?"

I'm confident I don't, but he picks up the pace, and everything starts to spin.

"I'm going to come." I couldn't stop this if I tried. My body has been primed first by Kane, then by Lan, and now it is ready for this rough fucking and everything else he does. Impossible though it seems, I am taking all of him.

My climax sideswipes me. My pussy locks over his hard length in pleasure on the cusp of pain. I groan and slam up against him, wanting more, needing to feel him even deeper.

He pauses to rise onto his knees, and taking my waist in his big hands, begins to slam me on and off his cock. I slip up and down over the bedding like a little rag tossed around in his hands. I stare at him through hooded eyes, trying to process what's happening. His long, sinuous tail curves around and over my thighs. The end can form a sharp point, but I realize he can retract this, leaving only a tufted end. It sweeps over my belly before wrapping around my waist. His hands slide all the way down my legs to my ankles…and then he lifts me.

My eyes roll back with pleasure as he uses his strong tail to shuttle me on and off his cock, while my legs are spread wide and up. The angle finds an entirely new spot that makes me twitch and buck. My pussy throbs and pulses as sensual delirium sweeps me along. I take in the image of the Devlin male—his strength, the straining muscles underneath his thick fur, his dark, intent expression, those wicked black horns, and the long tail wrapped around me.

"Tell me to breed you," he says.

"B-breed?"

"I am claiming you, although you will not be fully claimed until you take both my cocks, but that is only a matter of time. Tell me to breed you. Tell me to fill your needy little pussy up."

My jaw hangs slack. He could tell me anything right now, and it would only further arouse me. He places my bent legs over the crooks of his arms and leans down to take my lips in a hot kiss. His forked tongue thrusts in, and a strange spiciness fills my mouth. Heaviness rushes through me, followed by burning, languid pleasure. My nipples grow taut, and my pussy falls into climactic waves. I suck on his tongue as I clench over him.

He wrenches his lips from mine, tips his head back, and roars.

A hot flood fills me deep inside, and another spills over my belly. I'm still coming, spasming around his hard length. My skin is on fire, setting a mini explosion of pleasure over the surface of my skin.

He pulls out and flips me over onto my hands and knees.

"What-uhh!" His slick lower cock snags the entrance to

my pussy, and the other lines up with the entrance of my ass. I should be terrified, but I'm trapped under a blissful veil. I'm tingling inside my pussy, and even in my ass. When I glance down, I find my belly and thighs covered in black cum, the sight so confusing, I forget to be afraid of what he obviously intends.

His tail wraps around my waist, hands grasping my hips, and he slowly sinks in.

I groan. There is immense pressure, yet it doesn't hurt as he works his way in with shallow thrusts that grow deeper. "That's my good little pet," he says. "Now I shall claim you. I will fill your ass and hot cunt. I will seed you everywhere. I have marked you, have claimed you, and when I come in you fully like this, you will finally be mine."

Moaning helplessly, I push back for more.

He chuckles darkly.

"More," I beg, wanting him to fill this tingling void. My cries turn guttural as he works deeper. This sensation of being filled is oh so good. It burns and aches. He possesses me with his hands, his cocks, the surge and retreat, the rhythmic filling, the rippling of nerves as his bumpy cocks push in and out.

CHAPTER SIX

Kane

I realize that I cannot stay closeted in my quarters all day. The incessant beeping of my communicator confirms that it is so—Edicus demanding my presence.

I am lounging on Lan's makeshift bed, where my human captive is sucking my cock.

Erin was shy at first, but she is not shy anymore. My bonding essence that flooded my mouth when I first found her in this room also infuses the lubricant on my cocks. She has been licking and sucking them with greedy intent for the last hour, swapping from one to the other until it comes.

"I need to leave," I say, attempting to pry her from my upper cock. The lower one is half erect. At this rate, she will never be done.

She glares at me, grips the shaft in a most arresting way, and sucks me to the back of her throat, choking herself a little.

"Foolish pet," I say indulgently as I ease a finger into her mouth to pry her off. I have discovered that she is surprisingly fierce when she sets her mind to something. She manages to use her tongue to create a compelling vacuum as I seek to dislodge her. "Fuck!"

I come.

I am still coming as I pull her off, and it spews all over the fucking place. Black cum half drowns my wayward pet, dripping from her chin and nose to Lan's bed and liberally coating her throat. "Bad pet," I say, wagging a finger in her face.

Ignoring me, she licks around her lips and sighs with heavy contentment.

Mindful of Lan's prior warnings about managing women, I wish I had the time to discipline her, which I am still yet to do. Still, she is utterly adorable and proficient at sucking cocks, despite having only one mouth.

My communicator beeps again.

Avenged

I rise, setting the sweet human aside, who is eyeing my bobbing cocks with greedy interest. "Do not attempt to leave the room again," I say sternly, thrusting my legs into my armor and threading my tail through the flap. "You will be disciplined severely if I catch you tampering with the door lock again."

Her expression is guilty. At least I think it is a guilty expression. Still, it is hard to tell, given she is covered in my cum and busy stuffing fingers coated with it into her mouth, even as she glares.

As I thrust feet into boots and close the final clips on my armor, I decide I shall discipline her as soon as I return, just to be sure. Just thinking about applying my palm to her plump ass, imagining the wriggling and protests that are sure to follow as I set about mastering her, has my cocks rising in painful unison, trapped as they are behind my body armor.

I attempt to squeeze them into a better position to no avail. It doesn't help to cool my ardor when she stares with blatant interest at what I'm doing.

I leave before I fuck her. I want to fuck her all the time. It is the newness, I decide as I stalk along the corridors toward Edicus' commandeered office. I change my mind as I stop outside the door. Humans are just addictive.

Inside, I find Lan already present, filling all the space. On his knees to the right of the desk is one of the purple-skinned bastards. "You did not kill them all then?" I ask, pointing at the captive in question.

"What were you and Lan muttering about this morning?" Edicus says casually, ignoring my rhetorical question about the captive. He leans back in his chair and studies Lan and me through narrowed, calculating eyes.

Fuck! There is a reason Edicus is the leader of our pirate crew—he is fierce and misses absolutely nothing. Further, he likes to fucking play with you, lulling you into a false sense of safety when he is already on to you.

"Nothing." I mentally wince as the word leaves my lips.

Edicus looks from me to Lan again. I don't dare glance at Lan, who I suspect is looking guilty. He is the only one of us who could take Edicus out. Still, Lan was never much of a leader, nor does he have the lethalness that keeps us in business.

As my mind whirls over possible ways out of this mess, I realize that I do not have much time.

Erin

What the fuck is wrong with me? Am I under some sort of freaking spell? I need to escape. I need to get the hell off this ship when we arrive at the dock—I glance at my wrist piece—in mere hours.

My hands shake as I clean and gather my clothes, then throw things on one after another without conscious thought. Once dressed, I stomp back and forth by the bed.

They have gone, both of them. Will they be coming back soon? I don't know. Lan left for his shift, but Kane was summoned by Edicus.

Edicus is the real monster on the ship. Not Lan, who is sweet and gentle, as everything about our interactions tells me as much. Even Kane, while a monstrous Devlin and a pirate, is not wicked, nor has he hurt me once.

But they can't keep me safe. Neither of them can.

And even if they could, I can't live like this, lost under a sensual haze where I lose my fucking mind.

I need off this ship. Only I don't know where I should go now, nor how to hide for however many hours are left before we dock. Kane and Lan are sure to search for me, but they are hiding me and they won't be able to do so much longer without giving themselves away.

Escape hatches are positioned all over the ship, used for smuggling goods on and off. I could use one. Only the act of opening the door is terrifying. Kane told Edicus he jettisoned me out of the airlock. My former disguise is useless now. If they see the poisonous one, they will capture me again and take me straight to Edicus, but I also can't walk about as a human.

Discarding the goggles and mask, which make it hard to see, I put my jacket on and pull my hood forward, leaving my face in the shadows. It is the best I can do.

My room is not far from the escape hatch. But that probably wouldn't be the best idea. I could be trapped if they come looking for me.

I don't yet know where I'm going, only that I must move.

Taking a deep breath, I pop the door plate off and snap the cables together, wiggling them until the door opens with a hiss. The corridor is quiet, but voices are coming from the distance to my right. I turn left and take off at a run.

A cry goes up behind me. They have seen me.

"There she is," someone calls.

They did not use the word *it*. They used the term *she*. They are onto me.

I run faster and harder. My familiarity with the ship is my only advantage. I race down corridors, clamber up ladders and down stairwells, but their pursuit is relentless and they are gaining on me. When I turn the next corner, I find two more horned bastards in front of me.

"Got her," one calls, grasping my arm.

"She can run fast," one of those following says as they catch up. "Take her straight to Edicus. Best cuff her. I've heard about human females and the trouble they cause after Lan's many tales."

"Addictive, or so I heard," another one says.

I kick out and try to wrest my arm free, but they are

beastly and giant. The one holding my arm gives me a vigorous shake. "Quieten down, human."

My mouth dries up. I can't swallow nor can I get any words out. I sure as hell can't defend myself verbally or even physically. Using joined fists, I aim for the general area of his crotch, but his armor is fucking hard, and it likely hurts me more than him.

He chuckles and shakes me about again. "Little rebel has got some spirit. Edicus will like that. Either that, or he'll eject her out the airlock for sure this time."

The rest all laugh.

"No, he's not going to toss her out the airlock, look at her. Can't you smell her? Smells like raw lust. My cocks are fit to buckle my armor. More likely, Edicus will toss Lan and Kane out for trying to hide her."

I feel sick. I think I might be sick, but somehow, I swallow it down.

The beast picks me up like a bag of produce rather than a human, and with an arm anchored around my waist, carries me down the corridor. I wriggle and squirm. The method of transport does nothing to aid the sickness roiling in my gut.

We have not gone far before he enters a room and I'm dropped onto the floor. I glance up to my right, where Lan and Kane stand staring down at me with matching shocked expressions. Then to my left, where the stripy bastard who killed Mike lounges behind a sturdy table that once belonged to the former commander of our wannabe pirate brigade. He glares down at me before nodding his head at one of the men behind me. My hood is ripped off, and useless tears pool behind my eyes.

I'm a survivor. I don't fucking cry, but in this moment of darkness, I realize that I am doomed. The two males who helped me, Lan and Kane, are in trouble as a result. This is my end. It is their end too.

"Behave for your new master," Kane says ominously. "He will not harm you."

Edicus growls at Kane. "Do not fucking interfere. You're lucky you're not going out the fucking airlock." He scowls between them, rising from behind his desk, tail swishing. He is taller and broader than Kane, and his horns are immense. I have witnessed his violence. His power is unquestionable, as is his dominance here.

"Take her to my room," he says to the Devlin behind me, "and see that she is secured."

The Devlin male carries me out of the room. I think I'm going to be sick for sure this time. Miraculously, I'm not.

They take me to a spacious cabin, where they attach my bound wrists to a hook in the ceiling. There is a little slack, but the horned bastard, this one a dull gray with black stripes, presses a button on the wall. The chain rises, pulling my hands above my head, higher and higher, until I'm up on my tiptoes and swinging around.

Directly opposite where I hang is a huge bed.

"Behave, little human. Your master will be here soon."

He leaves, the door clicking shut upon him.

Fuck! I'm so fucked.

Kane

We are so fucked.

Silence follows the removal of the tiny human I had sought to claim as a mate.

"She's not yours anymore," Edicus says. "She is now mine."

His words bring a sharp rise to my chest. It takes everything I have not to allow my tail to swish.

"I ought to throw you out the airlock," he says, eyes narrowing upon us. "But she is human." His red gaze narrows upon Lan. "And I'm not the only one who has been subject to Lan's many colorful tales about the delights of human females. I can only think that she's addled both of your brains." He smirks. "Not that either of you had a lot to begin with. We are docking shortly, and there is still much to fucking move."

"Well, that is your own fucking fault for ejecting the purple bastards out the airlock," I say before glancing down at the last one, kneeling to his right. "Well, most of them."

Edicus turns toward the purple one. "He saw you take her to your room," the captive says. "I was watching the room."

My tail swishes as I fight the urge to let my claws spring out. I want to rip the little purple bastard's throat out and toss him out the airlock myself. The purple ones are loyal to Erin. Was he trying to save her? I believe that he was, and in doing so, has helped her capture.

Lan

Fuck! It has all gone fucking wrong, not that it was ever particularly right to begin with. The magnitude of our situation settles a weight upon my chest. I never really fit in with the pirates. It was just something to do. I like them, for the most part, especially Kane, who I consider my friend. I never liked Edicus. He is a vicious bastard, but he keeps the rest of the crew in line.

Now, a rage is building within me, one I have never experienced before.

Edicus give me a look, as if knowing all that I am thinking. "To the docking bay," he says. "Finish up the loading. We'll be landing soon."

"I don't like anything about this," I rumble at Kane as we exit the room.

"Neither do I," he says. "We need to get Erin the fuck out of here."

"I know we do," I agree. "But how? I can't believe you left her in the fucking room."

"Left?" He gives me an indecipherable look. Devlins are not known for subtle facial expressions. Most appear angry, even when they're not, and when they *are* angry, they look ready to maim you...which is not far from the truth. "You think she stayed in the room?"

"No."

I frown as that sets in. Erin would have almost certainly broken the lock.

"I got a call from Edicus," he continues. "I didn't have a fucking choice. I told her to behave and that I'd discipline her if I found out she'd misbehaved. Humans are every bit as tricky as you indicated. I wish I'd spent more time spanking her instead of fucking her."

A deep rumble emanates from my chest at the thought of disciplining Erin. My father always swore it was the only way to keep my mother from mischief. "How are we going to free her?"

"I don't fucking have a clue," Kane says. "But we must."

"Maybe she knows a way off the ship," I say.

"She will be locked in Edicus' room by now," Kane points out. His claws spring out unintentionally. "We both know what that means—he won't keep her there for long. Likely, she will soon be transferred to our ship. "

"That's probably our best opportunity," I say. "He will probably order someone to move her for him."

"Opportunity for what?" Kane asks as we enter the dock. There is still a fucking mountain of crates to move over before we dock.

"While he is moving her from this ship to ours," I answer.

"And what exactly are we going to do with her, assuming we get out of here?" he asks, rounding on me.

"I'm not sure about that part yet," I admit. "How much savings have you got?"

He flicks his tail as he grabs the first crate. I pick up one, two, and then three before hastening after him.

"A few thousand credits," he says. "How much have you got?"

"One and a half," I say. "Together, it's enough to buy a passage."

He sighs heavily and dumps his crate. I dump mine beside his and then follow him back for more. "We can't leave her with him."

"If we do this, there's no going back," Kane says.

"And you want to? Go back? What is back? Staying a pirate, you mean? I can't fucking bear to think of a woman, anyone with Edicus. You've claimed her, or tried to, but it won't make any difference. He'll use her until she has nothing left, until she is a shell. I like her…a lot." I think I fucking love her, but I don't say that part aloud. Is love even possible after only a few hours? More likely, it is a form of lust messing with my mind, as Edicus said. For all he is a bastard, he is not stupid.

Kane shares a look with me and picks up the next crate. I take two this time and follow him.

"We have enough funds to buy her passage. Erin is clever, I believe. All we need to do is get her to the passenger transport bay. They have ships going almost anywhere. Possibly, it's enough to get her back to Earth."

He huffs out of breath. "What the fuck do you know about Earth?"

"My mother came from there, for a start," I say, slamming my crates down with more force than is warranted before I follow him to collect more.

"Earth doesn't know the rest of the universe exists," he points out.

"There are still ways in. She'd be safe on Earth, with other humans."

"And we wouldn't be able to get her," he says. "Venturia would be better."

He's right. Also, much as I want her to be safe, I also want to claim her. "Venturia then," I agree.

I pick up three crates this time, and Kane picks up another one. His tail swishes, but inside, I believe Kane will do the right thing, the only thing.

"Fine," he says. "How the fuck are we going to do this?"

"The purple-skinned one," I say, nodding my head toward the dock door. "They are fucking loyal to her. They went to their fucking death to protect her. Free him, and he'll free her, if he can… They know the ship better than us. If there are ways out, he'll know it. Neither of us will be able to help her. Edicus will be sure to have guards on the door, but a sneaky little purple-skinned bastard, I reckon he could be allowed in."

He nods slowly. "It's the best plan we've got."

CHAPTER SEVEN

Five years later…

Kane

I dreamed about her again last night.

I used to dream about her every night, but it tapered off over time. It is strange how someone who passes through your life briefly can color it for many years. My life as a pirate is long behind me. I have a civilized occupation now. Well, one that involves killing for money. I'm a mercenary to be exact, but it is an honest occupation for an official company, and I can't go to jail.

I parted ways with Lan after we freed the tiny, non-poisonous being that turned out to be a human female. We left her with all our credit at the passenger transfer bay. Those places have more security than a Pomergorian battle cruiser, which is pretty much indestructible. She said she was going to Venturia, where the beings are diverse, and even humans can live in safety. Except I tried to track her down there a year later, when I had worked up enough credit, and she was long gone. I found out she'd transferred to an intergalactic hub, where the trail dried up.

For all I know, she could be on Earth.

If my dreams are any indication, that is precisely where she is.

I'd reconciled myself to Erin living her life. Then Avery Sinclair, the human god and writer, crashed into my new boss' life, and the dreams started again. Only they are different, lifelike, and I'm not the only one suffering this problem. Quinn, the Ravager, is having the same issues. Still, we both deal with it in entirely different ways.

The corridors of the fortress I now call home are black and unwelcoming, carved out of an icy mountain face. It's fucking freezing, and despite living here for the last five years, it still bothers me.

Not only me. When I arrive in the common room, I find Avery sitting at one of the long tables, buried in a thick, fur-trimmed crimson coat. Beside her is her looming life-mate, Haden, my boss.

Avenged

The common room is the hub of the mining operation, with tables and chairs in the center, a wall of food replicators on the left, and another area with low seating to the right. A vast, curving window offers views of the icy mountain range. I nod to Haden, although I'm wondering how I can broach the subject of my dream with Avery.

I elect to go and get a protein juice while I ponder the matter. I'm not very hungry, given I slaughtered a Narwan patrol group yesterday. They are grim, wooly insectoid adversaries but tasty when roasted. I kept one alive while I enjoyed a sample of his nest brothers. Given they are a highly intelligent species hell-bent on killing everyone in the base, I don't feel bad about my approach. I sent the survivor back with the message *fuck off, our claim* carved into its head.

As occupations go, I much prefer being a mercenary over space piracy. There is a lot more killing and a lot less lugging booty and the boredom of space. Now I get paid well to defend a highly lucrative mineral claim held by Haden's people, protecting it against the Narwan, who also exist on the planet.

No sooner do I collect my drink and return to the seats when Quinn arrives. He eyeballs Avery with the same reserve that I do. The tiny human has a filthy fucking mouth and is the definition of difficult. I thought I learned much about humans in my brief encounter with Erin. Still, over the last few months since Avery arrived, I have learned significantly more.

Quinn nods at me and stalks off to the replicator, doubtless ordering one of those broiled ratkins he loves. I shudder. It is a truly disgusting food source and makes me grateful I only need to venture here every few days to eat. "Did you dream of your human again?" I ask conversationally.

He drops his data tablet on the table and sits beside me. "Yeah. You?"

I nod and return my attention to my protein drink, which I am using as an excuse to venture to the common room.

Tension radiates from the big Ravager's body. I can tell Quinn wants to discuss the contents of his dream with Avery Sinclair, the writer who found a way to control the lives of everyone here in the mining colony of Xars.

Such matters are beyond my understanding, but in summary, the human writer was not merely writing but controlling the destiny of everyone here… Until Haden opened an intergalactic wormhole and commandeered both Avery and the computer she used to craft her stories.

I don't often try to grapple with the concept of the space-time continuum, but these strange and vivid dreams are forcing the matter. "Mine appears to come as a package deal," I say. "But I don't want the second one."

Avery's head snaps up, jaw hanging slack. Haden, attentive to his mate, reaches over to close her jaw. She scowls at me like it is my fault I am having the fucking dreams.

The arrival of the second, smaller human in the context of my dreams has caused a great deal of anxiety. "It is a tiny, noisy human," I continue. "It is always clinging and making demands. I do not want the smaller one. It is not very stable on its feet."

"You never mentioned this before!" Avery says, shooting daggers at me and clearly not remotely comforted by her mate's petting of her hair.

"I did not think it was important," I say with a shrug. "It looks small and deformed. Is there a way to get rid of it?"

Avery, who had snatched up her drink, spits it out.

"What? No!" She splutters, making like she is about to clamber over the table and assault me. I don't remember Erin being anywhere near this violent. Haden calmly snags his mate around the waist. "You are all fucking savages!" Avery rages. "That's a child. No, you cannot get rid of it! Do not dream about the mother again!"

I frown. "She is mated?" Betrayal is a sharp and insistent pressure at the base of my skull. It's so painful that I give little consideration to the struggle taking place on the other side of the table. For all he is a fierce warrior, Haden has poor control over his mate and has clearly not disciplined her anywhere near enough.

The replicator dings with Quinn's food order, but neither of us spares it a glance.

Devlin are hatched from an egg and emerge almost full size. I had forgotten that humans hold younglings in their bodies until birth. Little wonder it is so small. How would it even get out?

"A child? As in youngling? This cannot be right," I say, shaking my head slowly. I told myself that I was reconciled to Erin living her own life, yet murderous thoughts now consume me as I come to terms with another male breeding her. There will be dire consequences. "I have definitely seen the female self-pleasure, using a small pink magic wand. No female would do so if she had a mate. No wonder the youngling is so small and weak. It would be a blessing to ease its suffering." Only I'm no longer thinking of killing the tiny helpless being that I presumed to be a deformed pet, but the bastard who dared to put his cock inside my mate. I will take the mini human who is unstable, but my mate will need to be disciplined severely for that transgression. And I do not mean the Haden form of punishment, which we all know means fucking and is not a punishment at all. No, my little mate will find her bottom striped with welts as I lash her with my tail until she submits and accepts that she is mine.

"It's a fucking child, you moron!" Avery rants. "No, you can't ease its suffering! What do you even mean by ease its suffering? What the fuck is wrong with you? What the fuck is wrong with everybody here?"

The altercation ends when Haden stands, tossing his mate over his shoulder. He stabs a finger at me. "Do not mention the fucking Earth women again. See what you have done? Now I must punish my mate just to settle her down!"

"Your human management skills are lacking!" I mutter as he stalks for the door while his small, verbally offensive mate beats his back with her ineffective fists.

"This is not a punishment time!" she wails.

"It is always a punishment time," he counters as the door shuts behind them.

Everyone goes back to breakfast. It would be fair to assume myself and Quinn were not the only ones watching the show.

The replicator containing Quinn's food dings again behind us.

"She has anger management issues," I say, staring after the closed door. I'm confident I could do better with Erin, given Lan's many coaching sessions on human females. Lan… I have not thought about him in many years. I wonder what the ugly gargoyle is up to now. "I wonder if they all do?"

"No idea," Quinn says. Grabbing his broiled ratkin out of the replicator, he bites off the head and crunches it between his teeth before joining me again. "I'm a warrior. I've spent more time thinking about being with a human than is healthy." He holds out the ratkin body in my general direction.

I shudder and wave him away. I do not want to eat a

fresh ratkin, never mind a broiled one he has already taken a bite out of.

He scowls as though deeply offended by my rejection and takes another bite.

"Me too," I agree, returning to the matter at hand. "Given I cannot kill the small, deformed human that clings to mine, which Avery has indicated is a youngling, I'll have no choice but to take them both."

"You plan to claim her then?" he asks.

I don't answer him. I knew Erin for mere moments within a lifetime, but I have never forgotten her. It was the right thing to do, letting her leave.

Lately, I am less concerned about what is right or wrong.

Lately, my obsession with the delights of human females has returned in full force.

I had one once, and through necessity, let her go.

That will not happen again.

CHAPTER EIGHT

Erin

The years since I left piracy have not been easy. Not that I ever was a real pirate, but there was a point when I aspired to be. Then everything came crashing down when the Devlin warriors, the real pirates, infiltrated our ship. The subsequent events were crazy and remain hazy in my mind after all these years.

I ran. I thought it was the right thing to do—the only thing to do. They gave me credits. I'm grateful to them for that. I stayed on Venturia for a while, but I was hungry for Earth—the elusive place called where humans lived alone.

So I took a one-way ticket. With no intergalactic gateways to and from Earth, they basically smuggle you in and you're done.

I didn't realize I was pregnant, presuming space travel had upset my body. But there came a point where I realized something was wrong. Thankfully, I'd been given details of a medical facility on Earth to use immediately after arrival.

It still came as a shock to find out I was pregnant

I knew instantly the child was Kane's. I hadn't been with another male before or after. The doctor assured me everything was fine. The baby was humanoid and might not bear any Devlin features.

Then Brin arrived, and he was so beautiful. I wept when I first met him, because even though he appeared to be an entirely human baby, he reminded me of his father.

Brin looks nothing like Kane, with his pink skin, blond hair, electric blue eyes, and a beaming smile I never tire of seeing, even if he is always up to mischief. I can admit to disappointment in the privacy of my mind that he carried none of his father's genes, yet I was heartened he would fit in.

Only later, three years to be exact, his horns started to grow. Small bumps on his head made me worried he might have banged himself. They worried me more after several days of checking when they didn't disappear. Further, they grew and revealed themselves as the stubs of black horns.

Avenged

They are still tiny, and I can hide them under a baseball cap. His tail is another matter. It is already proportional to his body, long, black, and sinuous, which was bad enough until the blades at the end started to spring out. Mostly they stay inside, but they tend to pop out if he is excited or overtired. I've got many cuts from accidental lashings.

It upsets him when he hurts me, but he doesn't have full control. While his mind is quick, his body is a young child. How can I coach him when I don't have a tail myself? He doesn't like the tail being tucked away and complains and fidgets constantly whenever we go out.

I can't say I blame him, but what can I do? He's in danger from everyone, including other children at school.

As soon as the horns appeared, I tried to contact the doctor I'd used during my pregnancy, only to find the facility had mysteriously shut down two years earlier. It was a long shot, but maybe he knew of a way of getting back to Venturia, where my little boy could fit in and such things were accepted. I've scoured the internet for clues, for an alternative, but everything I find fills me with fear. Can I trust them, or should I steer clear? I'm not yet ready to risk my own life, never mind the precious life of my boy, finding someone to smuggle me from Earth again.

So here I am, trapped with a growing problem, although I can't bear to think of my son as a problem. His nature cannot be hidden forever, not easily, not without us retreating to a much more rural setting, and I simply don't have the money for that.

"Can I have an ice cream, Mommy?" he asks in his sweet voice. We don't leave our apartment often anymore, but he's got an active body and mind, and I try as often as I dare.

I smile down at him indulgently. He's a good boy, for the most part, if a little unorthodox at times.

"*Fuck!* Brin, no, sweetie, put your tail away."

"That was a curse word!" he announces gleefully.

"Mommy slipped up," I say, crouching so I can mask his lashing tail. I berate myself for the slip. Once a street rat and a pirate, always a street rat and a pirate. The familiar worry, that I am not a good mother and I'm failing on every front, resurfaces.

"Put the tail away, Brin," I say firmly. His lips quiver as it slithers back into his pants. I glance around the sidewalk surreptitiously while straightening out his jacket. No one's paying attention to us, thank goodness.

There are rare occasions when you can get away with it, such as Halloween and parties, although he hasn't been to a party in a while and I feel fucking guilty about that.

It's not only the tail I need to worry about, but the fangs and his growing horns, which I won't be able to hide under a cap forever. Then what will I do? I don't know the first thing about horns. Can I file them down? Would it hurt him if I did, or stunt their growth in some way? His horns are beautiful to me. They are part of him, part of his father, and

Avenged

I feel ill thinking that I might have to take drastic action for his protection.

I'm hanging on by a thread here, surviving day by day.

But I'm on my own. Where once I was coping, I'm not anymore. What if he gets sick? He seems so well and resilient compared to other children, from what I can tell, but I've no idea what to do for the best.

I'd barely come to know myself when motherhood was thrust upon me. Doing this alone with an alien baby makes everything so much more complex.

How do I get through this?

I don't have a fucking answer. I just want to keep Brin safe.

When I open my arms for a hug, he willingly comes in. He lets me know if he doesn't want to be hugged, but he's a tactile child and mostly enjoys cuddle time. "I love you, Mommy!"

"I love you too, baby bear," I say. "Come on." I rise. "Let's go and get an ice cream."

He whoops with excitement.

An ice cream vendor is at the bottom of our apartment block, with a few chairs and tables outside. He requests a scoop of chocolate chip, and we sit on the plastic chairs in the afternoon sun. My bright smile hides how I'm crumbling inside. I don't know how this story ends, but I have a terrible feeling it will end in tears.

I miss Brin's father and the beastly stone giant who was his best friend. I have thought about them over the years, a great deal at first, but less over time. As of late, I've been thinking about them more often. My baby is changing, and every day I look at him, I'm reminded of my past. I wish I'd stayed on Venturia. Returning to Earth was an impossible dream I found difficult to ignore, despite knowing it was a one-way ticket. It was also selfish and possibly tragic. Only time will tell.

"Let's head home," I say.

Brin has made a sticky mess of his fingers and the table. I grab a wipe from a bag, cleaning him up. Although he makes a fuss, he doesn't like sticky fingers, so he relents in the end.

The brief interlude of normality as we walk the short distance to our apartment entrance is ruined by a sensation of being watched. I throw a look over my shoulder, but I don't see anybody there. Perhaps I'm jumping at shadows. Every slip is a risk of detection. The fact the doctor who helped me exists here means someone knows about the connection between the worlds. Are there government agencies searching for interlopers? I suspect there are.

I swallow and quicken my steps, terrified of someone taking him from me, of them experimenting on him. The dread inspiring scenarios that might befall my baby bring a painful tightening in my chest. I don't know which way to turn for help, or if there's help at all.

It's a relief to be inside the apartment, although it brings a sense of being trapped. I peer through the curtains at the tree lined street below but see nothing obvious.

Brin takes out his Lego collection. He's creating a space station that is a scaled replica of a real one. If anyone ever came around, I'd have to pretend it was done by me! He's clever, ridiculously so. I had to take him out of school because he started asking the kind of questions that drew attention. I can't keep up with everything he reads on the internet. He knows more about biochemistry and tactical warfare than is healthy in a supposedly four-year-old boy. At the same time, he still appears so sweet and innocent.

We move regularly. It seems like the right thing to do. Officially, he's homeschooling. But he's growing and changing, and it's happening too fast.

I make a cup of tea while he is occupied with his Lego space station. The giant tub worth of bricks is scattered across the floor, and he is sorting it into piles, ready for the next construction phase. His tail has already wriggled out, and he uses it as an extra hand to help move his Lego bricks around. His cap is off, and I can see his horns peeking out of his thick blond hair. Here, he can be a little boy with a Devlin father. Here, he can be himself.

I turn back to my tea, only to grip the counter in shock as my mind is assaulted by the image of a longer, fluffier tail wrapping around my waist, slamming me on and off Kane's cock. My pussy clenches, and dampness gathers, along with a longing for a dominant alien who had confusing ideas about how to manage a human charge.

But he let me go, gave me his life savings, and risked himself so that I could be safe.

I would give anything to have him here with me.

The dreams have gotten worse of late. They're now so real, it almost feels like he's here, touching me. It's not healthy, but I'm stuck in a spiraling descent without a clue about what awaits me at the bottom.

Given I've not had a lot of luck in my short life, I can't help but fear the worst.

CHAPTER NINE

Kane

Troubles have ramped up on Xars since that ineffective conversation between Quinn and Avery, the god-turned-writer. The Narwan are making a big push, which means more killing for me. Unfortunately, it also means the lives of some of the engineers who work in our mine.

It's funny how circumstances change you from one role to another, from a pirate who discarded life without a second thought to someone who has a more tailored approach to killing. I never thought I'd care about anyone, yet I find myself strangely protective of the small, green engineers… Which takes my mind back to Erin and our fateful encounter after Edicus stormed her ship. Stealing from Edicus always ends poorly. As far as I know, he is still a pirate, still nefarious, and evades the law with ease. That's because he's clever and vicious, and he was made for pirating in deep space. I thought I was too, but perhaps not anymore. Now I'm a mercenary, and I'll admit, I like this role. Except the dreams are getting worse. They're visceral. I feel like I could reach through the void of space and time and touch her. Yet all I have done so far is follow her around like a crazed, spiritual stalker.

I wish I could do something more interesting…like fuck her? Only I don't fucking trust myself, not after what I saw.

As if my temper isn't frayed enough, I discovered a short time ago that Quinn had retrieved his human mate. How the fuck did he get her back here from Earth so quickly? He tried and failed to retrieve a genetic sample, which means he must have found another way.

The bastards are hiding something from me. They think I'm a cold killer. The truth is that I am, but deep inside, where my black heart beats, is a place reserved for a certain human. My soul, for want of a better term, belongs to Erin. She might as well be a god and creator like Avery, for she has claimed a part of me.

At least that was how it used to be, until my dream last night.

I will be avenged. I fluctuate between cold disbelief and simmering fury. If what I saw was real, as I think it is, then all prior mercy is null and void. Either another alien with a tail has fucked her, or I bred her and she fucking left with what was mine.

Only one person might give me the answers. Not Quinn, he's too busy fucking his now pregnant mate. Not Haden either, who has enough troubles of his own dealing with Avery, his small, verbally offensive mate. No, it's Layton, the green-skinned operational assistant who manages the work schedules…and other mysterious stuff pertaining to collecting human mates from Earth.

When I enter the operations room, Layton is not alone. Two engineers are gliding their small hands over the interactive consoles, checking the operation of the mine. They have special ledges built into the side of the sweeping desks so they can reach the surface.

"You're needed in sector two," Layton says, frowning at me. "What are you doing here?"

"Out," I mutter, glowering at the two small engineers. Their little bug eyes pop in their heads before they turn to Layton for direction.

"This isn't open to debate." I smile. It's not really a smile, more a show of teeth, but they get the idea. I've plastered on a civilized façade over the last five years since I arrived at Xars, but I'm not feeling civilized today. Layton nods like he's in charge, which I suppose he fucking is, and the engineers scurry out the door.

"I want to know."

He sighs heavily. "I can't keep sneaking people back and forth from Earth."

"So you do know how," I say, stepping forward, trying not to intimidate him because I want answers, but I dare say I am. My tail swishes from side to side, and I can't fucking help it. "I want her."

"And that is it," he says, folding his slender arms across his chest. "You want her, and so it must happen."

"Why not?" This sounds reasonable to me, especially given how she betrayed me.

"And what is she to you?"

"I mated her," I say. "I saved her."

His expression is insultingly skeptical as he raises both brows. "Maybe she changed her mind."

"She wouldn't," I say, more confidently than I feel. "He has a fucking tail!"

Layton blinks a few times, clearly confused by my random statement, which I admit *was* random.

"The child," I say. "The youngling Avery spoke about. He's got a fucking tail." I swallow. I don't know how fast human younglings grow, but he's not entirely human, is he? Devlins are born in an egg, and we hatch almost fully grown.

"You need to start from the beginning," Layton says. "This is highly irregular."

"Everything on this fucking base has been irregular since a certain writer turned up."

His lips tug up as he concedes with a smile. Then I tell him the story of how I met Erin, how she disguised herself as a poisonous one. How I saw through this disguise, claimed her, and finally, how I had to let her go.

"I followed her trail to Venturia, only to find she wasn't there. Gone to Earth, I was told. Then, after Avery arrived, I started to dream about her, just like Quinn dreams about Harper."

"They destroy the records of anyone who leaves for Earth." He nods thoughtfully. "You mentioned her youngling has a tail?"

"He does," I say. "But that's not the only problem,"

"Then what is?"

"Someone was following her. I only know because I was following her as well."

"You have dreams about her, and you merely follow her?" he asks, as though confused. "You don't touch her like Quinn did with his mate?"

My tail flicks from side to side, not liking where this is

going, not liking how he implies the connection to my mate is somehow inferior to the one Quinn and Harper share. "I have not, yet." I need to grow some fucking balls where Erin is concerned. My two cocks have all but shriveled up through lack of activity. I think they've forgotten how to work. I don't point any of this out. To be fair, Layton doesn't need the intimate details of my personal sex life, which is nonexistent, save for using my two hands. "I wasn't fucking ready to."

"Hmm," he says. "And someone is following her?"

"I believe so," I say, "He had a communicator in his ear. He was talking the whole fucking time. The boy—" I find the term strange on the tongue. I didn't even know what a boy was until I looked it up on the intergalactic web. "The youngling," I finally say. He clearly doesn't like to put his tail away. I can't imagine the indignity. It makes me bristle just thinking about it. "His tail came out. Erin was quick and tucked it back in, but it was obviously not some sort of fake toy. If someone is alert to such things… Perhaps their government is searching, or other unsavory types. I believe neither of them are safe." This is not only about Erin, although she's certainly a large fucking part of it. The child is mine, and she fucking took him from me. I'm sure of this, although he looks like his mother in every other way. The child who held her hand—the youngling, the boy, as the intergalactic web referred to him—is assuredly mine.

"And what are your intentions toward the mother?"

Now it is my turn to raise my fucking eyebrows. "Have I not made my intentions obvious? She is also mine."

He sighs heavily. "I'll need to clear this with Haden."

My tail lashes. I don't want any blocks. I don't want any reasons for this not to happen, but I concede. "It's possible, then, to go back there," I say. "Like Quinn did?"

"It is," he says. "But it is not easy. And it will need Haden's approval."

"Then we best get it," I say.

"This is getting ridiculous," Haden says, swiping a hand through his short hair after I explain my story for the second time today. We are gathered in the operational control room—Hayden, Layton, our green-skinned master of operations, Avery, Quinn, and me.

"Why are we discussing this?" Avery shoots a glare at her mate. "We can't keep absconding women every time an alien snaps his fingers. Also, he wanted to kill her child. He's a fucking savage. You are all fucking savages, but Kane is the most savage of you all!"

I blink a few times, my tail swishing as I take this in.

Haden's sigh is heavy, and I believe he is thinking about punishing her again. He is not the only one with punishment on his mind. Erin is due five years' worth of discipline. My palm will be ringing against her ass when I get my hands on her.

"I did not know it was her fucking youngling," I say. "Devlins emerge fully grown from an egg. I thought it was a pet."

"See? A savage!" Avery stabs a finger at me. She gets a spank for that. "He is still a fucking—Ouch!"

"Why exactly is Quinn here?" I ask, mostly to distract myself from thoughts of taking Erin in hand for her betrayal, of spanking her.

"I have experience in these matters," Quinn says, as though this were fucking obvious.

"He does. We both do." Haden says. "How do you think I got Avery back?"

A simple request has turned into a fucking committee. "So this wormhole—what do I need?"

"We will need all her details," Layton says.

"He won't have any details," Quinn says smugly, which is true. "He barely knows her."

The latter is not true, and I whip the cocky fucker with my tail.

He hisses. As he faces me, his claws spring out. "What the fuck was that for?"

"Still fucking savages," Avery mutters, distracting us from imminent battle.

"We are not all savages," Haden points out as though deeply offended, which is laughable, given he is no better than the rest of us.

Avery's snort is purely derisive. She gets another spank on her bottom. "Ow! Fuck!"

I consider pointing out that a light spank through layers of clothing will not offer much of a deterrent to Avery's combative behavior. Further, it will lead to the kind of trouble I find myself in. "You do not punish your mate nearly enough," I finally blurt out before I can better consider the merits of instructing another male. "Humans are both compelling and tricky. I am in this mess because I did not take the time to discipline mine before I was forced to smuggle her from the ship for her own safety."

Quinn chuckles. "I told him as much only yesterday."

"I am right here!" Avery says.

"Hush, mate," Haden says, voice low and rough. He closes his big hand around the front of her throat and pulls her back flush to his chest. It has an instant gentling effect upon Avery, who goes both still and quiet. I admit to being impressed and make a mental note of this technique, given I will imminently need to manage a mate of my own. It cannot hurt to have multiple approaches to the handling of humans.

"We will need whatever details you have," Layton says, returning our focus to the matter at hand. "Her name, age, location, and a detailed description of your human."

Description, check. But I only have half, and that was down to Lan. As for her age and her location, I don't have a fucking clue.

"He doesn't know," Avery says, tone dripping with snark. "Maybe she doesn't want to be found?"

"You really do need your punishment today," Haden quips.

"You need to speak to her, rather than just stalking her," Avery says, ignoring the threat emanating from Haden. "And how do you stalk her anyway?" She eyes me up and down. "You can't possibly be wandering around the streets of Earth looking like that."

Quinn snickers.

"Are you telling me you just fit in?" I challenge him.

"I fit in better than you," he says.

"You've got fucking horns!" I point out.

"And you've got fucking horns, fur, and a tail."

I cannot argue with this. "I don't think I have any substance," I admit. "I wasn't aware of my form or what I looked like. Nobody noticed me."

"It wasn't a two-way pull," Layton interjects.

"What exactly does that mean?"

"It means in Quinn's case, he shared the dream with his

mate. They were both aware of each other on Earth and here. Your mate does not appear to be aware of you. It is a one-way psychic connection. Sending you there…well, it could be dangerous in your current form, in any form to be honest. Intergalactic wormhole travel is, by nature, fraught with danger. And once there, it's not like you could disguise yourself as a human."

"Quinn disguised himself as a human?"

"Only one person saw me other than my mate," Quinn points out. "And nobody would believe that piece of shit."

I do not like the direction this is going, nor their implications that Erin might not want me, that our lack of a strong connection somehow indicates this will fail. "She is not safe," I say. "Our youngling is not safe."

"From whom?" Avery demands, losing all her former ridicule for my claim.

"Someone was following them—a man, watching them as he reported to someone via his communicator." I tap my ear. "The youngling let his tail out. I'm certain this man saw it."

"Boy," Avery says. "A young male human is called a boy. And this does worry me. There are rumors on Earth about agencies who have captured aliens. No one gave them much credence when I was there, but now, I can't help but wonder if they are true. Whatever happened between you and your former mate is between the two of you. But a half alien child…" She shakes her head slowly. "I'm terrified to think of him falling into the wrong hands. All this aside, I must be honest with you, Kane. I'm not feeling the story, and I need to. That is how I brought Quinn's mate, Harper, here—I wrote it in a story. A novella, actually, just for the two of them." There is no combat in her tone. The only emotion I sense is sadness. "I don't know how to make this work, or even if I should. It was different with Harper. She had read my books and connected to Quinn through them. I wrote his mate a place here on Xars, and well, the rest just happened. I just don't feel any kind of story or connection rising for you and Erin, nor for your child. I'm sorry."

Her genuineness is like a blow to the gut. Have I read this wrong? Is Erin with another alien male? Does she have another protector, leaving me superfluous to her story?

A blaring alarm shatters the quiet.

"There is an incident at the port," Layton says, frowning.

"What sort of fucking incident?" Haden asks. "Do we not have enough fucking troubles with the fucking Narwan and—"

"We need to send security there," Layton interrupts. "Promptly."

"I'll deal with it," Quinn says.

"I'll deal with it too," I say. "Then after, I would like to discuss this more."

I'm an undemanding male. I do my job and take my

money. I enjoy killing, and I kill the Narwan frequently. But the one time I need some help, the fucking station is going to hell. The sick churning in my gut tells me the matter with Erin is not yet over.

I hear the commotion as I push through the double doors, Quinn at my side, growling in anticipation of a fight.

"What the actual fuck?" Quinn says. "There are a dozen security personnel of various alien types around the perpetrator. They're shooting guns, but the bullets just bounce off."

I chuckle, all the tension leaving me, for I cannot help but think this is a sign.

Quinn cuts me a glare. "What the fuck? How can this be funny?"

"I know him," I say. "His name is Lan." I do not yet point out that he is Erin's other mate.

Lan

It's the story of my life that people shoot and ask questions later. Fortunately, my skin is near impenetrable, save for a shot from a blaster, and I rarely suffer more than a bruise. I want to spring my wings in a shield, but it can also be seen as a sign of aggression, so I don't.

Then one idiot at the back whips out a rocket-propelled

grenade launcher, and I know I'm fucked.

"Ceasefire!" a huge male with horns commands as he storms into the transport bay. The security guard holding the rocket-propelled grenade launcher swings his head at the barked command.

Unfortunately, his finger is already on the trigger, and he hits the launch.

The grenade shoots off of the loading bay floor, skittering along the ground and plowing into a tall stack of containers. They explode, sending a cloud of dust and debris whistling through the dock.

I duck.

"For fuck's sake!" somebody hollers—the horned male, I believe.

The rocket-propelled grenade launcher lowers, its owner looking sheepish.

So much for me making a quiet entry to Xars.

"Well, this is a fine fucking mess."

I turn toward the voice. Standing beside the huge male with the horns is another male with horns. This one has fur and a tail. Where once he wore the cobbled together combat armor of a pirate, now he wears a shiny black ensemble with a Xars Mining Inc. logo.

"Kane!" My face splits into a grin. The five years since I've seen him fade away, and I feel a strong urge to hug him.

He doesn't look huggable or approachable at all. His tail is swishing from side to side, and his lips are very thin.

"It wasn't my fault," I say.

"You are a gargoyle," he points out. "Everybody thinks you're coming for war."

"Hmm," I say, frowning. "I'm not a full gargoyle, though, am I? I'm only half."

"No one would tell by looking at you," Kane says, shaking his head slowly.

"Of course they would," I say, feeling deeply insulted. "I'm a buff gray at best. Gargoyles are dark gray, more often brown."

The male beside him begins to chuckle, and I like him already. He seems very friendly.

"He was being serious," Kane says to the horned male beside him.

The horned male chuckles harder. "An accidental comedian," he says. "And an accidental destroyer of docks."

Glancing over his shoulder, he hollers at a group standing about, eyeballing me like they think I'm about to start a war, which as Kane pointed out, my kind generally does. "Put the fucking fires out, idiots. What are you all waiting for?"

"I'm half human, and my name is Lan," I say.

"Quinn," the horned male says, nodding his head at me.

"So, how do you two know each other?" He swings a look between Kane, whose face has not softened a bit, and me.

My smile falters. From what I heard, Kane has been here five years and appears on friendly terms with Quinn, yet it is clear he has never mentioned me. I talk about Kane often and with admiration, but now I realize the feeling is not reciprocated. "We worked together to save a human, one we knew only briefly and who found a place in our hearts. At least I have a heart. I cannot speak for Kane." The anticipation I felt during the long journey here has already evaporated. "You have been here for five years," I finally blurt out. "Did you not mention me at all?"

Kane growls, and his tail lashing picks up pace. "I did not mention you," he says, "because I tried to put the past aside and not think about her, the non-poisonous female I could not have, even though I had claimed her.

I hadn't thought about it like that. Talking about Kane and Erin was the only way I could cope. I drove everyone crazy because I talked about them so often. "I've been dreaming about her," I say, because there are matters more important than Kane's feelings. "I think she is in trouble."

"Her?" Quinn muses, glancing between us. "I assume you are talking about Erin."

"I am," I say. "I did not get a chance to fully woo her, nor claim her, but it was understood when I offered up my life savings so she could be safe that she was both of ours. I would have given the money either way."

"Both," Quinn muses again, amusement in his voice and a broad grin on his face.

Kane sighs heavily, and the tension leaves his shoulders. "I'm glad you're here."

"It is?" Now I am confused.

"I also believe she is in trouble, and furthermore, that it will take both of us working together if we are ever to get her back from Earth."

My chest makes a sound like rocks knocking together. Some beasts call it a purr. In me, it indicates my approval of his decision, but it can also be happiness or contentment of some kind. I feel joy at the thought of Erin coming back into our lives. "I will do anything I can to help."

Kane's tail snakes out, and he whips the back of my legs. Despite having skin tough enough to stop a bullet, it fucking stings.

"I have not missed you," he says.

Contrary to his words, I believe that he has.

Kane

After Lan's arrival and a subsequent discussion with the fucking committee that my life is now subject to, some good decisions were made. At least I believe they were good decisions. Only time will tell.

I want her back, by whatever means necessary.

While I'm not entirely happy about Lan's arrival, perhaps I should have anticipated it.

Gods, goddesses, and deities in general are a mystical concept to me. I believe in life and death. Tonight, I'm ready to believe anything, if only it would bring Erin back. I must acknowledge what is going on, how Quinn was able to connect, communicate, touch, and by all accounts, fuck his mate, using nothing but the power of a dream. Well, not actually a dream, but an interdimensional portal that springs into effect when we lie down to rest.

The hows and whys are unimportant. I'm worried about Erin.

Nothing moves swiftly, since we don't have a surname. Even Lan doesn't have that, although he does have a little more information on where she lives. Like me, he has been dream-sharing, although he likewise hasn't touched her yet.

Tonight, as I lie in my bed, I'm restless and sleep will not come for me, no matter how desperately I want it.

I've been told that time moves differently on each side of the portal. Perhaps only minutes have passed for Erin, or perhaps several days.

I can't shake off the worry. It beats down upon me relentlessly from every direction.

Avery now feels a connection between Erin, Lan, and me. I have been told that her writing strengthens the interdimensional portal connecting Xars to Earth. She said she would think about us, and if possible, she would write.

CHAPTER TEN

Erin

Today has not been a good day, but sometimes, that's how it goes.

My journey into life on Earth has been a bit of a roller coaster. In my mind, Earth was utopia. I suppose compared to the shantytowns on the outskirts of Primus, it is certainly a different style, and it's strange to see only humans. I don't go hungry, which is really because of the credits I had left after my passage to Earth. Everything I had was converted to human money, which left me, while not wealthy, a long way from the poverty line.

After Brin was born, I worked for a little while, stacking shelves at a local homewares store. I even went out for coffee with a few mothers I met.

After my crazy life surviving on the streets, followed by years of piracy and my subsequent capture, I felt safe for the first time in my life. But change works in mysterious ways.

I missed Mike, the funny alien with too many folds of purple skin.

I missed the camaraderie I shared with my former pirate wannabe crew.

I was still sad and healing after the brutal way they were taken from me.

Sometimes, you don't appreciate what you have until you view it from the other side. I wouldn't have said my pirating days stood for much, but when I look back, I see they did.

Brin seemed to thrive at first, but he didn't know any other life. For his sake, I tried to make the best of what we had. But in traveling here, I had disconnected myself from everything that I knew. Earth was a one-way journey, and I understood that when I made the decision. Yet I also didn't appreciate what that meant, nor the consequence of my decision. Two years later, Brin started to change, and I realized my mistake was far graver than simply not fitting in.

Which brings me forward to today.

I haven't been out since the tail incident, but I'll need to soon. The feeling of being watched hasn't gone away. I feel desperate, sick, and unsettled, sinking under the weight of my doom. Last night, I dyed my mousy blonde hair darker using a box dye from my cupboard before cutting it.

I need to do the same to my son, but I can't quite bring myself to ruin his silky blond hair yet.

I tell myself I'm jumping at shadows, and then I tell myself I'm not being cautious enough. Doing this all alone is hard, and I end up second-guessing myself constantly, wondering if I'm doing the right or wrong thing and not knowing either way until it's already done. I don't want to uproot Brin again, but that's only one part of it. Every time we move, my money dwindles a little more. Finding work from home isn't easy, given my unique skills. Brin has insisted he can manage at home alone, and while I understand he's not a normal boy, I'm not prepared to take the risk.

I glance across at him. He's sprawled out on the rug, my old laptop in front of him as he researches something on the internet. I'm pretty sure he's bright enough for Mensa and would have a brilliant career ahead of him designing future space stations, if only he didn't have a tail and horns.

My prideful musing is cut off when a fat, fuzzy spider makes a sprint from the bottom of the window drapes directly for my son. I shudder. You meet some funky stuff in space. In my opinion, creatures with more than four legs have a superiority complex and an attitude to match. While

I know that Earth spiders don't carry blasters nor hatch galactic domination plans, they still give me the creeps. I'm caught between calling a warning to my son and searching for a bowl or box to trap it, when Brin's tail lashes to the side and spears the unfortunate spider…then he pops it into his mouth.

"What! Oh, no! Spit it out," I say, shoving my fingers into his mouth.

He spits out one leg. Like, where the freaking hell is the rest?

He meets my eyes and swallows.

Okay, ick, I now know where the rest is.

I'm at my wit's end.

I have an alien baby. He's growing too fast, and I can't hide what he is forever, and now he's spearing and chowing down spiders.

I burst out crying.

A small comforting hand presses lightly against my forearm. "I'm sorry, Mommy," Brin says. "I assessed it as a viable food source."

"It's okay, sweetie," I reply while still reeling at the *viable food source* statement. It's not even about the spider. For all I know, spiders are viable food. Only he can't do that sort of thing, not on Earth. A heavy awareness of time running out, of sand passing through an hourglass until only a few grains left, settles over me.

Kane

The smell of fuel assaults my nose. I blink a few times, taking in my location. It's nighttime. Tall buildings loom to either side of me, the brickwork in shades of brown and gray, with small windows, a few of which emit weak light. A faint misty drizzle settles over me, coating my armor, head, and horns. Beneath my booted feet is a poorly laid cobbled alleyway, glistening under a single yellow streetlight.

From the far end of the alley comes further light in a myriad of colors, along with the faint drone of engines as ground transportation pods zip one way or the other, their passage creating a whirling clatter as they rumble over the ground.

I am on Earth.

To my left is a metallic ladder, and my eyes follow the zigzag up the side of the building.

A rustle, dull clang, and grunt cause me to spin on the spot. A lone man sits enswathed in many layers of filthy clothing, emitting a ripe smell that competes with the reek of decay coming from the large rectangular construct to his right. Trash, I decide. He clutches a paper bag in his hand. Locking eyes with me, he lifts it to his lips and drinks liberally before pointing it in my direction.

Avenged

I shake my head, wondering if this is a human custom. Even at the risk of insulting him, I do not want whatever foul substance he has within that bag. The man takes another drink. From what I can tell, he doesn't seem intent on attacking me. In fact, he appears barely conscious.

I turn back toward the staircase, which looks flimsy. A Devlin is heavy compared to humans, but I believe it will hold me. She is up there—I can sense her. This will lead me to her and avoid detection.

The metal creaks ominously as I put my foot upon the first rung. After a few cautious steps, I feel confident that the staircase will not, in fact, crash to the ground. It creaks, groans, and rattles as I ascend, shaking ominously at one point, but holds.

Is death possible in this place? The metal feels real underneath my hands. The air is crisp and holds the stench of fuel. There is dampness upon my skin where it is exposed outside my armor. Essentially, everything about this feels real.

At the second to last set of windows before the top, I stop. Before me is a small landing and a door—*her* door.

When I test the primitive handle, I find it is locked. Erin is inside there. Only this flimsy door stands between us. I do not wish to break into her home, but I must get in. I crouch, putting my shoulder level with the upper part of the door, and push. The door creaks but holds. I note several resistance points. One at the top, one in the middle, and possibly another at the bottom.

Anticipating some noise, I draw back and then slam into the door.

It flies open with a crash.

I heave a breath, freezing in place.

"Keep the fucking noise down," someone calls, muffled through the wall…then all is quiet.

I push the broken door shut…or try to. The wood has warped, and I must use brute force to wedge it back into the gap.

Turning slowly, I rise, and my horns rake across the ceiling. "Fuck!" While attempting to dislodge my horns, my shoulder catches a cabinet hanging on the wall. Her dwelling is a strange, pokey little room with cupboards every-fucking-where. Easing around the cupboard, I bump into a small table with individual chairs placed around the edge.

The verbally aggressive neighbor thumps the wall and hollers muffled words at me.

A prickling sensation between my shoulder blades alerts me to her presence. I turn slowly, mindful of my horns and size within this tiny dwelling.

She stands in a doorway, weak light casting her in silhouette. The club-like weapon in her hand lowers, and her lips part on a soft gasp. She clamps her hand over her mouth like she seeks to prevent further noise from leaking out.

Perhaps the verbally offensive neighbor has been troubling her? I make a note to pay him a visit.

The pink clothing she wears clings to her slender curves and bears the picture of a rocket. Across her breasts reads a caption *Aliens do it better*, and below, *Ready for abduction*.

My brows pinch together, and my tail begins to lash from side to side. Is she fertile? Is this an invitation to other males to abscond with her?

If there is any breeding happening, it will be by me.

"Are you really here?"

Her soft voice is like a tiny fist that has reached into my chest and squeezed. If any doubts existed in my mind about whether we had bonded to her, they are over now. Her hair was short last time we met, and shorter still now, cropped close to her head and darker than I recall.

Mindful of the constrained environment, I get my lashing tail under control and step forward, setting the boards beneath my feet creaking under my passage.

"What are you doing here? How?" She shuts her mouth abruptly.

I want to touch her. I want to do a lot more than touch. "Where is he?" I demand, my voice a low rumble.

She backs up as I prowl toward her. "He?" she squeaks out.

"The youngling—child. Where is he?"

"Sleeping," she hisses, a little of her former fire entering her voice. She throws a telling look in the direction of the door to her left. "Although it is surely a miracle, given the noise you have made blundering into here. How did you even get here? What are you—Oh!"

Her rambling words are cut off as I close the distance between us and fist her slender arm.

The contact is shocking, and we suck in collective breaths. Chest heaving as I come to terms with the power of the moment, I pluck her weapon from her limp hold and prop it beside the door.

"The child is sleeping."

"That is good," I say. "You are long overdue your discipline, my non-poisonous little mate. It will be my pleasure to administer it, and then…"

CHAPTER ELEVEN

Erin

"And then?" Why am I asking what comes after? An alien male I last saw five years ago has just broken into my home and told me he will discipline me, and unlike all those previous occasions, this isn't a mere threat.

"And then I will fuck you," he says, voicing my prior fears.

Only it's not fear, is it? It's heated arousal, all mashed up with longing and a tender emotion that I can't quite place.

"Kane!" I hiss as he snatches me from my feet, then he ducks nearly in two so he can squeeze through my bedroom doorway before tossing me on the bed. The door shuts with a click. At least he didn't rip this one from the jamb.

"Quiet, tiny pet," he says in a deep rumble. "I should have done this before. Lan warned me about humans and their propensity for mischief. Likely, you would not have followed this foolish path had I disciplined you at the start."

Lethal claws spring out, shooting fear straight down my spine. A kind of cross wiring must have happened, because my womb clenches and a mini climax explodes deep inside me.

His nostrils flare, and his eyes take on a glint. "It seems discipline is very much part of human courtship, as Lan indicated."

I go to ask about Lan, the giant gargoyle who was so gentle with me, but the words get trapped in my throat as Kane takes a single claw and rakes it down the front of my nightgown.

"Who is the male you are seeking with this message?" he demands as he rips the gown from me and tosses it to the floor.

"Uh? Message?" Mental capacity abandons me, but it's little wonder, given there is a looming alien with horns and a built, fur covered body gazing with predatory interest at me.

He jerks his horns in the direction of the ruined nightgown. "You indicated you were ready to be claimed. Did you forget that I already claimed you?"

"I—" Nope, the words still won't come out. I giggle. It was the wrong thing to do. His eyes narrow in a menacing way that terrifies me this time before he flips me onto my belly.

"This will be a firm discipline. I suggest you find a means to stifle your cries, lest we disturb our youngling's sleep."

His big hand lands against my ass with a thunderous clap. The sting follows straight after, along with my gasp.

"Ow!" I arch up and throw a snarl over my shoulder at the big asshole who dares to spank me and further is making way more noise than I ever could. Fortunately, my sweet half alien baby sleeps like the dead, and nothing short of the building collapsing would rouse him. Possibly not even that.

"This is long overdue," Kane snaps back, landing another spank on the other cheek.

These are not playful spanks like I imagined when I read the books by Avery Sinclair. This is a sharp and relentless punishment that soon generates a stinging burn.

"I searched for you," he says between spanks.

"Worked and saved every credit I could until I had enough for passage to Venturia."

I squirm, trying to escape a particularly savage set of

spanks.

"But you had gone, fled where I could not fucking follow. And you took what was fucking mine."

His palm connects with one side and then the other, making me jerk and twitch and flight to get free. He is a brute and many times stronger than me. Subduing me so he can continue his discipline barely slows the process down.

"You are mine, little pet. You were the moment I thrust my primary cock into your hot, welcoming cunt and ass. I claimed all your holes, took you fully, planted my seed in your belly."

I clench with every clap of his hand against my heated flesh. I want to tell him that I regretted that reckless decision, that it was a low moment, a yearning for one thing like it might replace the desire for another. Our time together was short, yet I understood his character and integrity more thoroughly than some might in a lifetime when he chose to let me go.

When he chose my safety over his.

The pain morphs into a throb. This is Kane, the male I met so briefly, the father of my child, here with me, spanking me.

Mastering me.

Caring for me.

Emotions clatter together in my mind, ejecting a sob

from my lips. All the fears that had held me captive from the moment Brin started to change are liberated. He came. I don't know how or why, but I am so grateful.

It takes me long moments to realize that the spanking has stopped, that he has turned me over and is drawing me against the hard armor that covers his chest. "I missed you," I mumble, fingers fumbling, clumsy in my haste to find the closure mechanism so I can free him and feel the soft pelt that covers his belly and chest.

He helps me, seeming infected by the same fervor, jostling me as he unclips his armor all the way to his crotch.

I coo with joy as my hands worm into the gap and close over the silken fur. How can such a fierce male be so decadently soft? Like they have a mind of their own, my hands smooth down until they bump against his slick, ridged cocks.

He huffs a breath, then lets out a sexy growl that has my fingers curling tightly around the slippery flesh.

"Fuck!" He shifts, and the bed creaks ominously. I wriggle from his grasp, brushing tears from my hot cheeks before stuffing the nearest fat cock head into my mouth. The salty, spicy essence has an instant calming influence.

"Good pet," he says approvingly, fingers closing over the back of my neck, thumb brushing over the sensitive skin in a loving caress. "You will feel so much better once you get my seed into you."

I believe him. My mouth hollows around his flesh as I try to stuff him inside me as deeply as I can. My fingers wrap around his other cock, pumping in tandem with my bobbing head. Sucking up the leaking stickiness, I grow impatient for him to come, for this moment to be cemented, for the evidence that he still wants me, that he desires me, that he truly is here, the mate I have missed and longed for... that he is real.

"There is going to be a fucking lot," he mutters, his voice harsh and deep. "I have not spilled my seed for another since you left."

The magnitude of his words is lost under a hot deluge as he floods my mouth and sprays seed over my chest.

I suck it all down greedily. I've been under a shroud of fear and uncertainty for so long. I feel alive, and in the moment, I need so much more.

Kane

Her obvious joy in taking my seed into her goes some way to calming the beast raging inside me.

Some, but not completely. No, it has been five years—five years of searching, five years of feeling like I was missing a part of me, only to discover that she took not only herself from me, but a youngling that was mine.

I want to see him and learn about him, but I also want

to claim his mother because only through claiming Erin can I claim him too.

I thought I had made her mine once, but it seems I did not do a good enough job, and then circumstances separated us. I had no choice but to let her go, because releasing her was less painful than losing her to a monster like Edicus.

My mistake came in presuming our weak bond would bind us forever. This time, I must imprint myself upon her so that she understands unequivocally how she belongs to me.

I have just come all over her and down her throat. She is busy stuffing sticky fingers into her mouth, thrumming with pleasure. It pleases me to see my black seed upon her chin, the way her eyes turn hooded as it goes to work. It tempers the potency of my fury at seeing a blatant message upon her clothing. She betrayed me by leaving Venturia for Earth, where I could never reach her again.

The dark emotions festering within me have only one place to go.

A full claiming. Full, that's what Erin's going to be—full to fucking bursting with me.

She stills. I realize that I'm not purring anymore but growling, a rumble emanating from my chest that rattles with menace. She slowly extracts the fingers from her mouth and swallows.

The light source beside the bed is weak and leaves much of the room in shadow, which perfectly fits my mood. I appear calm, outside at least. My tail lashes around to land with a sharp spank against her ass. She jerks and eyes me nervously. I whip her with it again, causing her to gasp.

"Please," she says. "You've already spanked me!"

"I have not spanked you nearly enough." Only I don't spank her again. I roll, taking her under me, making the tiny human bed, which I fear might collapse at any moment, creak with the strain.

This won't fucking do at all.

I surge from the weak bed. My horns hit the ceiling again, but this time, I react faster and they only penetrate a bit. I snatch Erin from the bed, along with the soft mattress layer. The bed is thrust aside, and the mattress dropped to the floor. There is not a lot of fucking space in the room, but the floor at least feels sturdier than the flimsy framework the mattress was placed upon.

"What are you doing?!"

I do not take well to the censure in her voice and swat her pretty plump ass with my tail again.

Her squeal is choked off, and she throws a look toward the door as though fearing she will wake the child sleeping in the next room. My eyes narrow as I realize her desire not to betray what we do to our youngling provides opportunity.

"That stings," she hisses, rubbing her ass.

"Good," I say. "It was meant to."

She goes quiet, staring up at me as though seeing me for the first time. The effects of my seed are wearing off, and I very much like her renewed cognizance. Perhaps she senses that for all I am outwardly calm, I am a raging beast inside.

Taking her by the throat, I direct her to the center of the mattress, forcing her to her knees.

She doesn't move when I take my hand away. My cocks are long and thick with arousal, leaking lubricating oil she has no need for, if the glistening I see coating the tops of her slightly spread thighs is any indication.

Her hair was slightly longer last time we met, and I miss the advantage of using it as a leash with which I can direct her. No matter, there are other ways of subduing such a tiny being, of placing and controlling her for my pleasure.

Her eyes grow wide, lowering to where my cocks are partially hidden again behind the rigid armor. As I peel out of it, kick off my boots, and strip myself, she never looks away. I like her hungry eyes upon me, the submission of her kneeling pose, and the sense of power I command over her.

"This is the natural order of things," I say as I stare down at my mate, who dared to run from me. "You are small and weak. I am large and strong. I will protect you and our youngling. You will submit to my will. You will accept my needs. You will receive my seed as the gift it is and beg me for more."

She trembles faintly, chest heaving, even as she dares to avert her eyes.

I don't fucking like that. I don't like it at all. Sinking my knees into the mattress, I close my fingers around her slim throat and squeeze gently. Her eyes flash to meet mine, filled with a potent mixture of fire and wariness. Her thighs twitch together, and the perfume of her arousal saturates the air.

For all Erin was advertising for a male, I believe she is pleased that I answered her call. I will remind her thoroughly why and how she is mine.

I crowd over her, taking her down on her back. The bedding has gotten jumbled up and makes a pleasing nest of sorts.

"Now, I am going to breed you again, little human."

She squirms under my hold, and as my eyes lower, I note how her thighs have parted in invitation. I curl my fingers around her throat, applying a little pressure. "Be good and still for me, my little human pet, lest I damage your precious body. When you wriggle, it encourages my claws to spring out."

She freezes as my palm slides over the gentle swell of her belly before dipping into the slick folds of her pussy.

"God! What?"

Avenged

My fingertips find her pleasure nubbin hot, slippery, and already a little swollen. I pet it, watching her face contort, enjoying her breathy gasps. "Human females are made for pleasure. You have rejected me once as a mate, yet you cannot help but respond when I pet your pleasure nubbin. It is your downfall, and one I will exploit."

I circle it, tap it, and circle it again. She wriggles about, trying to escape my touch, wanting to deny my mastery over her, even as her breath stutters and her pussy becomes ever more slick with the evidence of her arousal.

I let myself sink, cataloging her every movement, allowing the rich scent to flood my senses.

My tongue swells, and the bitter taste of the bonding essence floods my mouth. I want to kiss her, but kissing her will potentially dull her pain receptors. I don't want anything to ease the coupling. When I take her, I want her to feel all of me inside her, every ridged inch.

"Do you want to come?"

She huffs out a breath, shooting daggers at me. "You know I do." I pet her needy nubbin. "Kane, please."

My lips tug up as I move my fingers from the temptation, petting the slick folds around her nubbin. "I like this begging, my naughty pet. But I own your pleasure, just as I own you. And you owe me five years' worth of begging and sweet climaxes that come only when I will it, so you are going to have to fucking wait."

Her eyes implore me as I take broader circles around her throbbing nubbin before pausing for a little tap where she wants my attention most. The whole area soon becomes plumper, growing *engorged*, as I pet all the way down and around the entrance to her hot, welcoming cunt. I like this very much. I didn't realize how her pussy could swell so perfectly, designed to hold a male's cock, or in my case cocks, both inside and outside.

Desperation is written in every contoured line of her face.

"I'm going to inspect you," I say.

She blinks. "Inspect?"

"You did not yield to my claim last time," I say, circling her pussy with a slowness that is inadequate to get her off. She dances her hips to the side, trying to take control.

Growling, I tighten my fingers on her throat. I wish I had some fucking binding, but my tail will have to do. I loop it up and around, slipping it under her back, curling it around her to pin her still.

She groans. I think my runaway mate likes being restrained.

I have been avoiding her hot little cunt, but I can't resist it anymore. Slowly, I sink a single finger into her gripping heat, and now it is my fucking turn to groan. Humans are addictive. I defy an alien of any kind not to fall under their spell. I work it in and out a little before pressing a second finger inside. A jolt runs through her body.

"You will take both my cocks here."

She shakes her head.

"Yes," I counter, thrusting my fingers in and out, delighting in the wet squelchy sound they make.

Her breathing turns to a ragged pant as I finger fuck her, shifting the angle of my hand so that my palm slaps against her swollen pleasure nubbin with each deep thrust.

A flush spreads over her cheeks, throat, and across her tits. She's going to come, only I don't want her to come. She doesn't fucking deserve it.

I stop.

"What? No, please. God, please!" She blinks a few times, disorientated as I line up my cocks, smearing black pre-cum all over her flushed pussy.

My balls ache. It doesn't matter that I just came down her throat. I need to seed her and breed her more than I need my next breath.

Grasping both my cocks in one hand, I squeeze them together, line up with her cunt, and sink slowly in.

Erin

I didn't think a person could be this aroused and not actually come. My entire pussy throbs, and rabid desperation crawls under my skin. I know what's coming next. He has told me in clear, unambiguous terms.

I can feel him pressing against the entrance of my pussy, sinking a little way inside. It's not just one cock, but both. Can I take both? Am I ready? My body may never be.

But damn, it feels so good to be helpless before him, with his tail lashed around my waist. I have literally nowhere to go.

When his claws are retracted, the tips of his fingers are soft and round, but tonight, the claws have come out a tiny bit and add a little bite where they depress my flesh. I should be terrified, but I'm not. I want him, this fierce alien male who claimed me and, due to circumstances, was forced to let me go.

Bearing his child, seeing him reflected in my changing son every day, I have thought about Kane often, missed both him and the pleasure he wrested from my body in our brief interlude.

But this? I'm questioning if I can take this.

He's not giving me any choice, and besides, he has teased me to the point of madness and I'm freaking desperate to come.

But that also presents a problem. If I weren't so aroused, this might go easier for me, but I am swollen, and there's no space inside for his two massive cocks.

My mouth hangs open, and I pant like I'm running for

my life. My eyes lower to where our bodies press together, mine human, pale and small, his huge, fur covered power. He holds his cocks squashed together and thrusts a little way inside. He eases just the tips in and out. The stretch is alarming and enticing. I'm only a human, and my body was not designed for this.

"Relax for me, little pet," he says.

The words soften me in more ways than one. They take me back to when we first met and Brin was conceived. I ought to be insulted, yet they are more of a caress. Why are humans so highly coveted in the universe, when we are so unremarkable?

Tonight, I don't care why, I'm only glad that we are.

I groan.

He sinks deeper, setting all the nerves in my channel flaring to life. The image we make is debauched—a giant alien male twice my size hovering over me, intent on filling me with his inhuman cocks. I can't wriggle away. I can't move between his big hands and the long tail wrapped around my waist. It aches, but strangely, it doesn't hurt at all, more a dark, twisty kind of pleasure that stokes memories.

The sounds escaping my lips turn guttural, and then he is there, kissing me, filling my mouth with a strange spice that sets pinpricks dancing across my skin. He is inside me, I realize, all the way inside, so deep. My nipples peak where they brush against his fur. His strength is staggering as he raises to his knees and slams me on and off his cocks. My clit throbs where he pounds against it. My pussy becomes a source of fiery pleasure, my breathing turns choppy, and my heart is thudding out of my chest.

I need to come.

I need to come so badly.

I need to come, or I'm going to die.

I come. It rolls through me like a dark mystical wave, a rising, tumbling pleasure that picks me up and rips me apart.

When I wake up, Kane is gone. I push the cover back slowly, forcing myself to sit up and staring around the room like he might be hiding, as ridiculous as that is.

The sharp, achy feeling deep in my pussy brings a flashback of him impaling me with both his cocks. I lower a shaking hand, fingers dipping into the stickiness before lifting them up.

Black seed coats my fingers.

It wasn't a dream. A person can only do so much with an alien dildo toy in their sleep.

It wasn't my toy. From what I can see, it's still safely locked inside my drawer. Kane was really here, in my bed, and he fucked me, then he left.

Not my bed, I reflect as I look around. My room is half

dismantled, the bed frame over to one side and the mattress on the floor!

With a growl of annoyance, I haul my ass out of bed, thoroughly exhausted and disgruntled with my lot.

Then, as I stand up, wavering, body suffering from the pounding by his two cocks, I just feel fucking sad. I never got a chance to tell him about the danger myself and Brin are in. Worse, he has fucked me, and for all I know, I'm now carrying another alien baby.

The backs of my eyes sting as I snatch my robe from the back of the door and drag it on. I will not fucking cry. Not now, not ever. I need to be strong.

It's then, in my moment of weakness, that I hear murmurs coming from the lounge. Brin must be up and watching something on YouTube, probably a quantum physics lecture, knowing my son.

Squaring my shoulders, I muster the will to pretend that everything is okay and throw open my bedroom door.

I scream.

Two sets of eyes turn my way.

One set are electric blue in an angelic face with blond hair…and black horns.

The other set are red in an inhuman face covered in white fur…with black horns.

I blink a few times. The vision does not go away.

"What the f-udge are you doing here?" I hiss, rounding on Kane.

"Conversing with my youngling," he says as though this is fucking reasonable. "We are discussing tail etiquette."

"Tail what?" I am physically not at my best, and my mental capacity is equally limited.

"Mommy doesn't like to talk much until she's had her coffee," my sweet son chirps.

It's then that it hits me how close they are together, how utterly unafraid my son is by this huge alien male, how Kane's tail has curved protectively around him.

"We are designing an intergalactic transponder!" Brin continues proudly.

Nope, I definitely need a coffee. A lot of coffee.

"It is a basic design but well thought out," Kane says. "I have given him a couple of pointers."

"What the hell do you know about intergalactic transmitters?" I hiss before I can think better.

"I know a lot about transmitters," Kane says. Narrowing his eyes at me, he unwraps his tail and raises with the feline grace of a predator to his feet.

I huff out a dismissive breath. "Really, a space pirate turned transmitter designer?" I scoff.

"So we are going there," he says, rounding on me. "Were you not also a space pirate, mate?"

"Mommy was a space pirate? Cool!"

Belatedly, I realize this is the first mommy-daddy argument my son has ever witnessed, and furthermore, he has just discovered I was a space pirate. We never broached his obvious strangeness, not once. I haven't moved, and Kane's tail snakes around my waist, tugging me against his huge armor covered body with alarming ease.

"I, ah, don't think this is an appropriate conversation in front of a child."

"Devlin hatch fully grown," Kane says, hooded eyes zoning in on where my dressing gown has parted. "While Brin is physically a youngling, his mind is fully developed and has been for a while."

CHAPTER TWELVE

Erin

"I need to make a coffee," I say, changing tact and giving a pointed look towards the kitchen.

Kane's chin lifts, and he looks over the top of my head as if confused.

"It's a drink," I say.

He nods and unleashes his tail from around me. My son, who has the brain of a super physicist and, according to Kane, is an adult in every other way, watches us with interest.

No, I can't quite wrap my head around that. Taking hold of Kane's hand, I drag him in the direction of the kitchen. "How are you going to get us out of here?" I demand the moment we are a short distance away from my son. Kane is staring at our joined hands, his impossibly large and mine tiny by comparison.

He lifts my hand up and inspects it, carefully moving each finger and then gathering the whole thing up within his hands as though it were the most precious thing in the world. I feel uncomfortable. No, not uncomfortable. *Aroused* is the word I'm looking for.

Kane's eyes lift to meet mine, and heat ramps up, making my pussy clench in a painful way, given all we did last night. His nostrils flare, and he crowds me back against the cabinet. I can't gauge his intentions, given he is fully clothed, although I cannot see holding him back for long should he have a mind.

"Not in front of Brin," I hiss.

His eyes narrow. "I was not going to couple with you." He releases my hand and stabs a finger in our son's direction. "Also, while he may physically be a youngling, he understands everything. He heard my arrival last night and realized who I was."

"How could he? How could he possibly realize who and what you were?"

"He peeked out his door, saw my tail and the rest of me.

I nodded in acknowledgment, and he showed no sign of fear. Younglings always recognize their brood fathers. We are a warring race. Recognizing your brood parents prevents accidental killing." He shrugs like this is no big deal.

I'm blinking and trying to make sense of what he said. I can't. "How are you going to get us out? Are you still a pirate?" I never saw Kane the day the last member of Mike's crew got me out of the ship, but I understood he burned bridges, and further, gave up his life savings so I could be safe.

"I haven't been a pirate since your liberation from Edicus. I have a real job now as security at a mining site." He takes a half step back. "And I don't know if I can get you out."

I'm confused by him having a 'real job' because—and this is judgmental of me—he really doesn't look like the kind of alien to patrol a mine site making sure no one tries to steal a pick. That's what mining security personnel do, right? "What do you mean, you don't know if you can get us out?"

"I mean I do not know."

"Well how did you get here?"

"Through an interdimensional portal."

"A what?"

"Our son will explain."

He will?! "So why can't we go back the same way?" I glance toward my son, who is doubtless listening in, despite appearing occupied.

"It is dangerous," Kane says.

"And it is dangerous for us to stay here," I say, my frustration rising.

"I understand, and I do not like the situation either, but I now live light years away and there is no two-way passage between Earth and there. You realized that when you got on the transit at Venturia. Taking you back will not be simple."

"Are you stuck here too?" I ask. Much as I feel safer having Kane around, he can never step outside the house, and what am I even going to feed him?

"I'm not trapped here," he says.

I shake my head slowly.

"I'm having a dream," he elaborates, making everything clear as fucking mud.

"That doesn't sound very scientific," I say, thinking it actually sounds crazy.

He shrugs. "The nuances of time and space are beyond my understanding. There's a human female among us. Her name is Avery Sinclair. She was a writer from Earth."

"She writes stories about a planet called Xars," I interrupt.

"You've read her books?"

"I do. I picked one up in a second-hand bookstore last week. I've only read a couple chapters. I haven't had the time. "

"You should read the books," he says, taking a step forward, hands braced on either side of me on the counter, before he stoops and lowers his head until it is almost level with mine. "All of them. And if a new one comes out, you especially need to read that."

My mouth opens and closes again. "This is sounding less and less scientific. How will reading a book help?"

"It will help," he says, and then he is gone.

"Don't worry," my son says as I stare around the room in shock.

"He said he would be back."

"The intergalactic portal he uses is unstable. That's why I'm making a transmitter. I've ordered all the parts from Amazon. They should be here today."

Just another day in the life of my extraordinary child. "Okay. Please let me get a coffee."

My son giggles and goes back to his laptop. I make coffee. My hands shake so badly that I spill coffee all over the side, but I persevere, needing something to get me through the rest of the day. As I take my first sip, a thought comes to me. "Where did you get the money from?"

He gives me a shifty look. "I used your credit card."

Only now—as I look at my son with his sweet, angelic face, his black horns that have grown more than I might have wished for, and the tail, which pokes out a hole in his pajama bottoms—do I realize he does not sound like a four-year-old boy. Well, he sounds like one in terms of the pitch of his voice, but based on his sentence construction and word choice, he definitely doesn't.

He shrugs when I continue to stare at him, seeing him clearly for the first time. "I did not want to upset you. I realized you were already upset about my chosen areas of study. I was going to tell you the rest."

"When?" I croak out.

"Eventually. I was waiting for the right time."

"And this transmitter will allow us to speak to Kane?"

"Yes," he says. "Once I have completed the construct. Kane gave me the signature for Xars, and I should be able to lock into it. Given the distance, I'm going to have to bounce off amplifier stations."

I nod before taking another sip of my coffee. "Did you realize someone was following us?" I'm still struggling to process that he is effectively an adult in a child's body, but I must.

"Not at first," he says. "I didn't mean to let my tail out.

My mind may be mature, but my body is four years old. My tail gets itchy and uncomfortable and lashes out sometimes."

It breaks my heart to hear him say this, to hear the slight catch in his voice, like he feels bad for being a child. And while I understand Brin is physically a child, his mental development is somewhere else.

"I need a cuddle," I say, putting my empty coffee cup on the counter.

He doesn't hesitate to come into my arms and accept my need for connection. I don't remember having cuddles when I was his age. I remember coldness and barely enough warmth from a blanket.

"Does Kane cuddle you?"

I choke out a laugh. "He does."

"And Lan?"

"Lan?" I ask, my voice a high squeak.

"Your other mate. Kane spoke of him."

"What exactly did Kane say about Lan?" My mind is reeling, and my heart is thudding like I've just run up the freaking stairs.

"He said he was also your mate and a gargoyle. I'm excited to meet him. He sounds cool."

Brin does not seem fazed by my second mate. I didn't realize I had a second mate, given Lan and I never shared full intimacy. Still, I understand we would have, had circumstances not parted us.

"He is a gentler mate," I say. "I dare say he will be happy to cuddle you as well."

"And is he really as big as Kane says, and near indestructible?"

"He is," I say.

"Will you tell me about your life as a space pirate while I work on the transmitter," he says. "I'd like to know more. I never asked before because I could see it was difficult for you. There were times when you would be distant, not from me but just from life in general. You were thinking about them and about your past. I wanted to know. The time was never right, but today, I think it is."

"I will," I say. "But I also need you to order me something else from Amazon."

"What's that?" he asks.

"All the books by Avery Sinclair."

CHAPTER THIRTEEN

Kane

I wake up with a roar, chest rising unsteadily as I gulp deep breaths. I was not ready to return, yet here I am, in my bed back on Xars. That wasn't enough time to see Erin and Brin, my son. I've spent the last five years fixated on finding Erin and reclaiming my mate. Younglings were a consideration too far ahead.

I wanted her. I wanted to breed her, but I didn't think I'd had enough time. The feelings consuming me contain both pride and fear—pride in my son's captivating presence and intelligence, and fear because he is encased in a frail human body.

For all he has horns and a tail, they are poor weapons on one so small and physically a youngling. He's not a Devlin. He's something else, a wondrous product of our coupling.

Brin cannot hope to protect himself or his mother, who is entirely human, small, and weak. I've seen enough of their kind. She has no weapons, no gun with which to defend herself. Though she spent many years living among the purple folded ones, before that she was in a place where her skin gathered all those scars. In the pale lamplight of her room, it was possible to forget about them.

Erin's life has been harsh, but danger is not done with her yet.

We needed to talk about why she left Venturia. Did she realize she was pregnant at the time? It seems unlikely. Raising an alien child on a planet that pretends the rest of the universe does not exist would have been foolhardy.

I don't have the answers. I only know I imprinted myself upon her fully last night.

Then this morning, I was snatched away.

My stomach rumbles. This space traveling business has left me depleted. I dress efficiently in my armor before storming down the passage. I tap my communicator, and my ears meet Layton's calming voice, which does fuck all to calm me. "Good morning, Devlin warrior," he says.

"Where is she?" I demand.

"If you're asking about Avery, she's in the common room with Lan."

"Why isn't she writing?"

"Perhaps you would like to discuss why Avery is not writing with her mate."

Okay, that was a little bold on my part. I just want Avery to write the fucking book. I just want Erin to have a reason to be here. As I push through the double doors to the common room, I find it packed. A shift must have just ended, because the place is full of small, green-skinned engineers.

I nearly trip over one. They move with alarming speed and are not always easy to notice, given they are so low to the ground.

"Watch it, big foot!" one of them calls.

I am deeply insulted by his comment, until I look down and realize that I do, in fact, have big feet compared to his tiny form.

"My feet are not big," I call after him. "It is you who are unnaturally small."

He doesn't mind me, but none of them do. They are industrious beings who have witnessed how I fight to protect them, despite their poor sense of humor.

When I was a pirate, nobody cheered on my killing, save my brethren, who might offer a nod of acknowledgment if

Avenged

I performed a particularly impressive kill. The green-skinned engineers who work here cheer me daily as I emerge from the tunnels after slaying the Narwan. I admit, I enjoy being on the side of good, whereas once, I was on the side of evil and corruption. Here, on this strange ice planet, I have found my place, only something is missing, and until that missing piece is here, I cannot possibly be complete.

My focus centers on the table where Avery sits with Lan. Whatever Lan just said must be amusing, because Avery throws her head back and fucking laughs. I storm over, not sure of my intentions but definitely angry.

"What the fuck is so funny?" I demand.

Avery sobers immediately. Lan raises an eyebrow.

"We were talking about Erin," Lan says. "About how she broke the lock and escaped your room."

"Don't you have books to write?" I ask Avery.

Avery squares her shoulders. She is an indomitable human and is cowed by absolutely nothing, not even the threat of her mate's punishment.

"I have written a lot," she says. She indicates Lan. "We were talking more about Erin before I write again."

I feel a little churlish. Avery is only doing research so she can better write Erin into our lives.

"You are late this morning," she says, eyeing me as she

picks up a piece of toast.

I never quite got my head around toast, and I have no context for it. It comes out of the food-bator whole in this form, dripping with a strange oily substance. I'd rather eat roasted Narwan any day, but the toast makes Avery happy. Given she is such a combative female, Haden should feed it to her all the time. I take a seat opposite them. "I dreamed of Erin last night. I was with her."

Avery puts her toast down and sits very straight. "What happened? What did you tell her? Does she know she's in danger? How was she?"

I rub the fur on the back of my neck. "We did not discuss matters in much detail. She seemed well. The youngling was well. He's a fine child. His brain is mature, although his body is immature."

Avery's face softens. "Oh! How wonderful. I'm so glad you had a chance to meet him. What did Erin say about the people who were following her? Does she know who it is?"

"We, um…we didn't exactly discuss that part in detail."

"Why not?" she demands.

"Yes. Why not?" Lan also demands.

"Also, that is the most important fucking part," Avery says. "How can I ever write this into a book without the details?"

"Well, maybe she doesn't fucking know either," I say.

"She's better placed than us," Avery points out. "How long were you with her? Did the portal pull you back?"

"We were discussing other things," I say, feeling deeply uncomfortable. I'm not proud that I fucked Erin when I should have been discussing the threats.

"You fucked her, didn't you?" Lan says, glaring at me across the table and looking like he's ready to thump me.

"I might have done so," I say defensively. "I fully intended to talk to her and then I was distracted," I admit. "I thought there would be more time."

"Well don't be fucking distracted," Lan says. "This is her life we're talking about."

"I know," I say. I feel like the lowest form of being. "You said yourself that humans are addictive and tricky."

"You're trying to say she tricked you into fucking her?" Lan says.

"Well, actually she did. She was wearing clothing with a spaceship on it. It was a blatant advertisement for a male to fuck her."

Avery bursts out laughing.

I glare at her, confused. "Where is Haden?" I ask pointedly.

"Oh no," she says. "You don't get to use Haden against me. And now I'm intrigued. How is a picture of a spaceship an advertisement for an alien male?"

"It said *Aliens do it better*," I say. I feel prideful, given I am the only alien who has fucked her. "And at the bottom, it said *Ready for abduction*. If that is not an advertisement for an alien mate, I do not know what is."

Avery bursts out laughing. She laughs so hard, she has to hold her stomach. I do not think this is a good sign. Is she hysterical? Is there some loophole in the intergalactic portal that I do not know about?

She shakes her head. "Oh, Kane, that is just a silly Earth saying. It doesn't mean anything. Erin was definitely not trying to get an alien to abduct her."

"She was not?" Lan asks, clearly as confused as me.

"No," she says. "She was not."

I feel a little foolish now, given what I did, how I impaled her on both my cocks. She winced a little the following day. I'm sure she must be sore.

"I'm not convinced about that," Lan says.

"Lan," she says, patting his arm affectionately. "Trust me on this. This is not an advertisement for an alien abduction. If it were, women would be abducted all the time."

"How do you know they're not?" Lan asks seriously.

"Trust me," she says. "They are not. Anyway, what did you discuss while you were with her? Did you discuss anything?" She looks skeptical at this point.

"My son is building an intergalactic transmitter so that we can talk. While it will take some time, he is progressing well."

"That's amazing," she says. "It also means we can ask Erin questions without distractions." She gives me a pointed glare. "If either of you get to be with her again in your dreams before I finish this novel so we can properly bring her here, then for goodness' sake, talk to her. This is not the time for fucking. Really, it's not."

CHAPTER FOURTEEN

Erin

My son has maxed out the credit card, and I can't even find the will to care. My time on Earth is ending, one way or another. I forgot to tell Kane about the man following us, which is ridiculous when I've been so worried about it and after what I assumed when he broke in last night.

It's too late now. First, I was shocked by his arrival, then distracted by his attention, but I can't allow myself to become distracted again, not when Brin's life is at risk. I'm no stranger to conflict after surviving for years on the streets, but I'm alone here, and I don't stand a chance.

I need Brin to finish the transmitter for both our sakes, so I accept the endless stream of delivery people bringing parts to my door. Each time I open the door with trepidation at first, then there's relief when I find a man with a parcel.

I pass these off to Brin, who takes them to his room…because he says I make too much noise and distract him.

He's been in there all day and has all the parts he needs now. I take him food and drinks regularly. I can't help him with this, yet I still worry about him as though he is a small boy.

"I've finished," he announces, emerging from his room as the day draws to a close. "I'm going to start testing."

"Tomorrow, love," I say, pushing the silky hair back from his forehead. I admire his horns. "The human is the weak part of you, but your body and your mind, even if it's more developed, both need to rest."

He nods and yawns heavily. "I know," he says. "Tomorrow, I'll start testing."

He neatly packs his stuff away and hops up into bed. I kiss his forehead as I pull the covers up, which seems silly now I know he's all grown up.

Gently closing his door, I turn…and swallow down a scream. "What are you doing here?" I hiss. "How is the floor even bearing your weight?" As Lan moves an inch, the floor creaks ominously. "How much do you weigh?"

He shrugs. The floor creaks again. "Not sure," he says. "About as much as a regular gargoyle."

"Oh my god, you're going to go through the floor. Sit down—no, lie down. We need to distribute the weight."

He chuckles, which sounds like rocks rumbling together. I check my son's door. He needs to rest. He's never going to sleep if he discovers there's a gargoyle in his home.

"It will hold," Lan says. "I've walked all the way over here from the window, although I might have bent a few of the steps on the way up."

"Steps? You came up the fire escape?" I turn toward the emergency door to find it hanging off the hinges.

"I did," he says. "I wouldn't recommend using them now."

"Oh my god! What if there's a fire?"

He takes a step toward me. It sounds like someone dropping a hefty weight from an enormous height with every step.

"It'll hold," he says. "The stairs held. Mostly. A few of the brackets came out a bit. It's at a bit of a precarious angle now, but I guess in an emergency, people could sort of get out."

I rake my fingers through my short hair, grip as best I

can, and give a sharp tug.

"Please stop moving," I say. Only Lan doesn't stop, and he walks all the way over to me and picks me up.

"What? Why would you pick me up? That's putting even more weight in the same place."

He chuckles. "You weigh almost nothing. I can't see how it'll make much difference, but if it pleases you, I'll sit."

He does sit…with me on him. The floor creaks. I admit there are pieces of furniture that are heavier than a human, perhaps. Still, he's very concentrated and solid and warm to the touch, and he has a pleasant if strangely dusty smell that tickles my nose and distracts me. I'd forgotten many aspects of Lan, including how gently he holds me. He is nothing like Kane.

I sigh and release the tension that is gripping my body.

He hasn't gone through the floor yet, and I figure he probably won't. I rest my head against his chest, which emits a strange rumble. It sounds like tiny stones rattling together, almost like a purr.

His wings, which he mostly keeps tight against his back, spring, curving protectively around us both, and I feel like I'm being sheltered from the storm of my life.

"I've missed you," I say.

"I missed you more," he says.

I puff out a little breath. "How could you possibly

know?"

"I know," he says.

"Did you get here the same way Kane did?"

"Yes," he says. "I went to sleep, and then I was here. I've been thinking about you all day. I spoke to Avery about you."

"Avery Sinclair?" My head pops up. "The writer? Is she really writing a book for me?"

"She is," he says, wings snapping shut against his back. "She's halfway through, from what I last heard."

"I've been reading about Xars all day," I say. "In between deliveries."

"That's good," he says. "You need to."

"What about Brin?" I ask. "Won't he need to read it too?"

He shrugs. "Avery only indicated that you should read it."

"This all sounds very mysterious."

"Yeah," he agrees. "Um…may I inspect you?"

"I, ah, don't think this is an inspection time."

"I believe any time is a viable inspection time if the subject agrees. Are you in agreement? Would you let me…would you allow me to inspect you now?"

I feel a catch deep in my chest, my heart opening for this

strange, earnest gargoyle, who, while looking like a gargoyle, is nothing like them in any other way. Gargoyles have a reputation for war, but as I sit within the cage of Lan's arms, I'm reminded of how things were between us last time we met, how during the nights afterward, I dreamed about his gentle inspection, and how my life has been poorer without him.

His presence here erases the distance of five years. Everything I thought and felt about him is precisely the same.

"Yes," I say, the word tumbling out before the consequence can register.

I'm expecting him to go to my bedroom. Instead, he rises and shuffles forward until he reaches my kitchen counter, where he drops me.

My thighs spread wide around this thick waist. "I don't think this is—"

His fingers grasp the bottom of my T-shirt. Ripping it over my head, he tosses it to the floor, inflaming a sense of urgency within me. I feel hot. My pussy clenches sharply. While I'm sore after what Kane did yesterday, an electric current runs through me, driving any caution away. Nothing matters in this heightened state besides completing what Lan and I started all those years ago.

This feels right on every level. I need Lan and to be

connected to him, and only then will I be complete…and safe.

He emits a deep rumbly growl of frustration as his thick fingers fumble with my bra. I take over, and it follows my T-shirt to the floor.

"I need you naked so I can thoroughly inspect you," he mumbles, grasping the waist of my leggings. He pulls them down, nearly dislodging me from the counter in his enthusiasm. His plans to strip me are thwarted by my sneakers. He grumbles a deep rumbling sound that makes me giggle.

He glares at me, jaw set in a stern line that only makes me laugh harder. He tugs defiantly, ripping sneakers, pants, and panties from me and tossing them to the floor.

I'm naked, and I'm also wildly excited. How is it possible to be this aroused so quickly? His mere presence is acting as a powerful aphrodisiac.

He grasps my ankles in his big hands and tips me back. I squeak, elbows hitting the counter behind me.

"What are you—Oh!" My eyes cross as his tongue, the instrument of my destruction, swipes over my pussy. It's big, broad, and has a slight roughness that feels freaking amazing against my most intimate place. There were nights when I lay in bed and convinced myself it was not as good as my memories portrayed.

It was, and it is.

Avenged

I'm soon seeing stars as each leisurely lick sweeps up and catches my clit. My pussy throbs and squeezes over nothing in anticipation, then I'm rocketing straight into space.

I come embarrassingly swiftly.

He surges up, wiping his mouth with the back of one hand as he reaches for the fastening of his pants with the other.

My body may be singing, but I'm not mentally ready. "I'm not... I don't think..." I stare blatantly at his busy hands at his waist, hoping it's going to be a manageable size, yet terrified that it might not be.

I suck a sharp breath in as his buckle comes free, and he shucks his pants down to hang at his thighs. I shake my head. My pussy clenches violently with a mixture of fear and unhealthy fascination. The pre-cum leaking from the tip is clear, which comes as a relief after Kane. His cock is a deep plum red, and the surface is lumpy. Nothing about the length or girth looks out of place in his hand.

I swallow.

Okay, I want this, I really do, but I can't see how.

He appears to be coming to the same conclusion because he looks from his cock to my pussy and back again. He frowns and, using his forefinger and thumb, pulls my pussy open.

I try telling myself that I've had a child, but to be blunt, that fucking hurt. While his cock isn't that big, it is thick, really freaking thick, and my spiraling thoughts can't decide whether or not he is thicker than both of Kane's cocks. He might be. He might not. I'm too busy hyperventilating, and my vision is coming through a tunnel.

Oblivious to my chaotic mental state, he lines the tip up with my entrance and takes my hips in his hands.

Then he's pushing, and I'm squirming, and despite his bruising grip, my pussy is on lockdown and he's not getting very far.

"You're very fucking wet," he mutters, his face a picture of concentration. "How can you be so fucking wet and I still can't get in?"

It's a rhetorical question. He doesn't pause his attempt to bludgeon his way into me to check for an answer. I think about answering anyway, pointing out that he has a cock the size of my baseball bat and how I never once contemplated sitting on that.

But I don't. I'm too busy squirming and remembering to breathe and not freak out. The sensations are interesting and frightening and enticing as he slides in and out a small way.

"Fuck," he says with a grunt, wings springing in a great *whoosh*. "Fuck, I'm not going to fucking last."

His hands are shaking where he holds me, so huge they grasp most of my lower body and ass as his hips thrust shallowly. My pussy clenches, relaxes, and clenches again. Everything gets muddled up in my mind and body as the nerves he reaches flare to alert.

I want to feel him. I want to be complete, to join with Lan in this intimate way.

"Oh god!" He shifts one hand, and a broad thumb smashes down over my clit. I jolt. My pussy squeezes his cockhead in a vise. "Oh god. Don't do that."

"I must, or I will never get fucking in," he says. "Come, little human. It will help to loosen you up."

I'm not convinced about this logic, but he swipes his thumb back and forth over my clit regardless. He's far too rough, but I'm swollen and sensitive, and my rising arousal distracts me from his attempts to penetrate me with his monstrous cock. I can't focus on everything. My mind splits between the two sources of stimulation—the surge and retreat as he tries to impale me, and his petting of my oversensitive clit. All the little neurons are firing, and I can't decide whether I love it or hate it, but I definitely want to come.

Propped on my elbows, I can't tear my eyes away from what he's doing to me, and I watch, slack-jawed, as the massive male shuttles his monstrous cock ever deeper into me.

I'm so full, yet half of him is left out. But heaven help me, the pressure and pleasure are the darkest, most twisted kind.

As is inevitable that I climax around him in sudden,

sharp, rhythmic waves. The vision of him almost to the root as I clench over him is utterly depraved.

He grunts and stills, and I feel the first hot jets bathe the entrance to my womb. A deep rumble emanates from his chest, and his hips jerk, wedging him a little farther as yet more of his hot seed fills me. Having nowhere to go, it leaks around his cock and drips to the floor as he rocks.

"Fuck!" he mutters gruffly.

My pussy won't stop clenching, and I'm so out of it that I literally see stars. I swear, the top of my head is itching, his cock is that deep inside me.

He moves both hands back to my hips, grips, and pulls out, only to slam all the way in.

He must have anticipated my scream because he clamps a hand over my mouth. His eyes clash with mine, and my pussy falls into a spasming frenzy as my inner muscles try to eject his cock. They can't. He's wedged deep, and I have no choice but to accept. Long moments pass before I calm down enough to realize I'm not broken—stuffed beyond capacity, but not broken.

Lan grunts as my pussy decides to clamp down extra tight.

He peels his fingers from my mouth slowly. "Are you well?"

I glare at him. "No, I am not fucking well. I've... You've..."

He makes the rock rumble, and his eyes lower. I can't look. I can feel it. The visual evidence is going to freak me out.

"I couldn't help myself," he says, rocking his hips to ease his monster cock in and out.

The sounds that tear from my lips are those of an animal. He clamps a hand over my mouth again and finds my clit with his thumb. I'm stretched obscenely around him, and his rough petting makes everything lock up harder.

I shake my head and glare at him.

His determined expression does not bode well for me.

Don't come, don't come, I chant over and over.

My prayers go unanswered as he continues to slowly fuck me.

"I need to mate you," he says, expression darkening in a way I've never seen on him before.

I can't...I can't come like this. I can't.

But he doesn't stop. He is relentless. His concentration is absolute. "Come," he says. "Squeeze my cock. I want you to. It's going to feel so fucking good."

I shake my head, but I'm coming. I can't stop it. I can't prevent it. He's working my clit relentlessly, and my pussy is absolutely stuffed.

My climax comes like a distant train upon a track heading toward me in slow, steady increments, rising, pulling, drawing ever closer to the point of no return. The first contractions are both agonizing and so pleasurable, and my cries turn from guttural, to hoarse, to begging him to stop, to begging for more.

He stills deep, grinding against me, flooding me once again. He rumbles deep in his chest, his dark eyes glistening with an inhuman zeal.

"Mated," he says. "Now, we are mated."

CHAPTER FITHTEEN

Lan

I cannot say I care for the intergalactic portal that takes me to Erin. It is cold and empty, like a void. You question your sanity while you are lost in its oily embrace. My time with Erin is too brief before I am snatched away again.

Still, I am part of this now. There is no disputing my claim.

I cannot keep the fucking smile off my face as I breeze into the common room, where Kane indicated he was eating breakfast.

"You fucked her," he says, eyes narrowing on me.

"I claimed her," I counter.

"Claimed means fucked." Rising from his chair, he promptly whips me with his tail.

"What the fuck? Don't do that."

He whips me again. "I will whip you as many times as I fucking choose. What did you find out?"

"Find out," I repeat.

"Fuck!" He whips me once again. "The agency. The watchers. Does she know who the fuck they are?"

"I-I—" I stammer like a buffoon. "I didn't ask," I finally admit.

"So you just fucked her?" He whips me yet again.

"I will rip your fucking tail off if you dare to whip me one more time."

His nostrils flare with defiance, and he whips me once again.

"What's going on here?" Quinn demands as he stalks over to stand beside us.

"He fucked her," Kane rumbles, stabbing a finger in my face. At least he didn't fucking whip me this time.

"And this is a problem?" Quinn asks. "I thought you fucked her? I thought you were both intending to fuck her? Why are we discussing this?"

Kane growls again, deep and full of aggression. It makes me deeply uncomfortable. I think I'd rather he whipped me than make this horrible growl. It's the kind of sound he makes just before he maims or kills things. Or kills and eats them. Would he eat me after killing me? I believe I would not taste good.

I blink a few times realizing I've gotten distracted.

Quinn and Kane are still waiting for an answer.

"She is in danger, and I should have been focusing on that," I admit.

"Hmmm," Quinn says noncommittally, putting his big hands on his hips. "You dream shared with her last night then?"

"I did."

The glow I earlier experienced ebbs. This is not about me claiming her. This is about keeping Erin safe. Not only her, but her youngling. I lost sight of my real mission and failed. My earlier elation wanes, leaving only shame.

"They are addictive," Kane says with a shrug of his shoulders.

"They are," Quinn agrees. "You can be forgiven for being distracted in her presence after such a long time."

Only I don't think I can forgive myself if anything happens to her because I was thinking with my cock. "I should have asked her," I say

"You should," Kane agrees. "Did you learn anything at all?"

I shift uncomfortably. I learned she has the tightest pussy in the universe and to thrust my cock in and out of her and fill her with my seed is a torturous kind of heaven. I don't mention this. Bringing Kane's focus to how much I enjoyed Erin's pussy would not be helpful. If anything, I believe it would be detrimental and likely to result in Kane whipping me again. The way his tail lashes suggests he is already thinking along these lines.

"Have either of you spoken to Avery today?" Quinn asks.

"No," we both say in unison.

"Hmmm," Quinn says again. "It is a risk sending either of you in a way other than a dream, unless Layton works out a way to transfer you into an alternate body."

"How is he going with that?" Kane asks.

"Slow." Quinn shrugs.

"What alternate body?" I ask, looking between the two of them. "I didn't hear anything about this."

"Too busy napping by the sounds of it," Kane says.

He's still pissed. He's probably right to be pissed.

"And Layton can do that?" I ask. "Put us into another body?"

"You're broken up into particles," Kane says. "It stands

to reason that you can put the particles back together in any way you might choose."

I shudder. "You mean make me into a human?"

"That is the general idea," Quinn says. "You will have the same mass, so you would be a very" —he gives me an up and down look— "dense human."

"I cannot imagine not having a tail," Kane says, still flicking his tail as though agitated by the mere thought of losing it. "I think I would keep trying to move it and then be disappointed when I found out it wasn't there."

"That's really a minor consideration," Quinn says.

Kane gives him a look.

Mine and Kane's communicators bleep.

It's Layton, and he has an update for us.

CHAPTER SIXTEEN

Erin

I thought I was in a rough state after Kane, but today is a thousand times worse. Like Kane, Lan's arrival was as swift as his disappearance. Now he is gone, once more into the void of space.

I shower, dress, and put the coffee on before poking my head into my son's bedroom. I find him up and busy at the electronic assembly on his desk, which has a computer tablet built into the front. He has a keyboard in one hand and is tapping away with a speed that defies logic.

It looks impressive. I mean, it's a transmitter, but the

apparent complexity of Brin's homemade device is blowing my mind. If I had any doubts that he was mentally an adult, even though he appears to be a small boy, they are over now.

"My transmitter is nearly ready, Mommy," he says excitedly. I still struggle with his childish voice uttering adult statements.

"So I see, sweetie," I say. Should I call him sweetie? Should I be calling him Brin now?

"I like sweetie," he says like he's reading my damn mind. Can he read minds? Some aliens can. Can Kane read my mind?

"You're thinking very hard about something, Mommy," he points out.

"Ah, um, can you read minds?"

He shakes his head, grinning. "No, I can't read minds, and neither can Kane or Lan, although he projects his emotions a lot."

I blink a couple of times. "What sort of emotions?"

"He loves you," Brin says. "Very deeply."

"Okay, I kind of sensed that. Anything, err, else?" I feel deeply uncomfortable asking this question. I certainly don't want him to know what we were doing last night.

"No, only emotions."

My eyes narrow. "What about Kane?"

He shrugs. "Devlins don't really do emotions in the same way. They experience more of a..." He pauses a while, as if searching for the right words. "A deep primal obsession. You are his. I am also his."

I'm trying to work out whether I need this kind of enlightenment before coffee when the transmitter splutters static. Brin instantly turns back and starts tapping away on his keyboard.

"I'm getting closer," he says. "There's a good chance I'm going to connect today."

I'm interrupted from this exciting news by a knock on the door. "Are you expecting any more parts?" I frown between my son and his scientific assembly.

"No," he says, hitting a button on the pad, which powers his transmitter down. "I have everything I need. No more deliveries are due."

"Do you remember what we talked about?"

He nods.

Another pounding comes from the front door, the impatient kind you don't usually get from delivery drivers, who try once then dump and run.

"You need to hide." Am I overreacting? Possibly. Yet the tingly awareness coursing down my spine is poking at my fight-or-flight instincts.

There is nowhere to flee. If it is who I think it is, they will have already covered the fire escape, even assuming I was ready to kill myself trying to get down that deathtrap. It wasn't great before Kane and Lan stomped all over it with their heavy alien weight.

I'm distracted from my mounting terror when my son taps a button, and the transmitter transforms before my eyes into… a Lego Death Star.

I blink a few times. "How did you do that?"

He shrugs. "Caution seemed appropriate."

Okay, I can't get my head around that right now. I stare around the room a little mindlessly, looking for a place for him to hide. When I glance back, he's gone.

"Brin!"

Another firmer knock sounds on the door.

"I'm still here, Mommy." When I turn toward the voice, I see his chair move, followed by the sound of his feet pattering across the floor. "I'm hiding like you asked."

"How long have you been able to do that?" I ask weakly.

"A while," he admits.

The next thud on the front door is louder still and accompanied by a shout, "Open up!"

I want to discuss this. I want to do many things, but people are thumping on my door, and I need to deal with that.

"I'm going to answer the door," I say. It might be a delivery driver my son forgot about, or something innocent that has nothing to do with a delivery, but every instinct inside me says it's not. "Whatever happens, stay hidden if you can. Stay safe. Mommy loves you." I can't see Brin, and I wish I could judge the worry on his sweet face.

"I know," he replies.

I wish I could hide too, but I can't and it's better that I answer them than they bust it down.

I think about picking up the bat as I close his bedroom door softly. Something tells me it's not going to help me. A sick premonition washes over me as I go through the motions of undoing the locks.

An army sweeps past me as it opens, men in combat gear and balaclavas brandishing machine guns that bowl straight over me. "What the h—" I'm slammed up against the wall, knocking the air out of me. I'm flipped around to face the wall, arms pulled painfully into the small of my back and restraints snapped around my wrists. "Take your hands off me! What is this about?"

Fisting my arm, the soldier turns me back around. More men surge into the apartment, throwing doors open and ransacking rooms, opening drawers, and tossing contents onto the floor randomly.

"What the hell are you doing? What are you looking for?"

Avenged

I've been so busy watching the thugs with weapons storm around my home with my heart in my mouth that I don't notice the suited one until he stands right in front of me. A pinched face without a trace of joy inspects me through black-rimmed glasses. "Where is he?" His calm voice is somehow more terrifying than if he had shouted.

There are two men in my son's room, and I can hear them tossing stuff about. If they touch the Death Star, try to pick it up or touch it, will they realize what it is?

"Where is your son?" He punctuates each word, stepping closer, getting into my space.

I back up to the soldier behind me. "He's gone."

"Gone where?"

"How would I fucking know?"

The slap takes my head on a journey that leaves my ears ringing. I suck in a sharp breath, tasting blood in my mouth.

This is only the beginning. He's offering me a sample of what I can expect if I don't cooperate. But I'm a street rat who grew up on Primus, and he's going to have to dig deeper if he wants to break me. I've no doubt he is determined, but so am I. Worse is coming. I understand this, but I don't want it to happen in front of my son.

Blood trickles down my chin. "You have no right. Get out of my house."

"We'll leave your house when we're ready," the cold man

in charge says.

My possessions are being tossed everywhere with a desperate kind of fervor. Furniture is overturned, the cushions sliced down the middle, and the stuffing ripped out. How swiftly it is turned from a regular home to a place of decimation is unreal.

My heart is hammering a mile a minute in my chest the longer it goes on. Fear they will discover either Brin or the transmitter beats down on me. I remind myself that while he might appear a child, he's a mature half alien who can build a transmitter out of parts he bought on Amazon, and further, can turn invisible.

I'm still frantic. What if they have some sort of infrared detectors that reveal his heat signature? I can't see any evidence. They are just thugs with weapons searching the place.

"Nothing!" comes a chorus of calls as the men emerge from first my room, then Brin's, and then the kitchen area.

The man in glasses, who appears to be in charge, stares down at me. He nods. "Seal the place off. Keep a team on the fire escape, just in case. Organize an inspection crew asap. I want this apartment gutted, floorboards up, and every scanner we have deployed. The full analysis."

I do my best not to turn back as I am thrust out the door and frog-marched down the corridor. As I reach the end where the elevator bank resides, I do take a final look to see them taping up the door with a police warning. Two men stay behind, bracing the door.

The elevator arrives and takes me down and out onto the street. Here, I'm bundled up into the back of a blacked out van.

I'm shaking. I'm terrified for myself, but I'm more terrified for my son.

CHAPTER SEVENTEEN

Kane

An urgent call sees us head for the operational center with all haste. Several green engineers are present, working at the console when I arrive. Avery, Hayden, Quinn, Lan, and I gather around the console.

"We just got a message from Brin," Layton says.

"You did? What did he say?"

"The message is coming over a considerable distance," Layton says patiently as the small engineers slide their fingers relentlessly over the interactive surface.

The speaker crackles, and then a sweet, young voice that belongs to a fully developed Devlin disguised as a human child comes through. "…in the…"

"Brin! It's Kane."

"Daddy!" His excited, childlike voice speaking that word hits me like a physical blow. The word was not a familiar one to me, but after he used it last time we met, I looked it up on the intergalactic web. My chest swells with pride, knowing it is an Earth term used to refer to their male brood parent.

"They took Mommy!"

All joy is gone. The statement fills me with pain not unlike a Narwan pincer stabbing me in the gut.

"Where are you? Are you safe?"

"I'm safe. I can make myself invisible, so I hid. They work for the Bureau of Extraterrestrial Control, and I overheard them talking. They are bringing back equipment that I won't be able to hide from."

"Invisible?" I say slowly as I try to take all this in. Pride rouses in my chest once again, but it is tempered by the knowledge that this bureau has their hands on my mate.

"Who took Erin?" I ask. "Was it the bureau?"

"Yes! They hurt her, tied her hands up, then they took her away!"

My nostrils flare, and Lan makes an aggressive sound of rocks knocking together in his chest. "We're going to get you out," I say before turning to Layton. "Can you lock on to his location?"

He nods and motions to the small engineers, who are busy at the console.

"I'm not leaving!" Brin announces. "I need to help you get Mommy. I know where she's been taken."

"Good," I say. "You are helping by coming here, where it is safe." The engineers remain busy, and I know they are working to bring my youngling through the wormhole. I need to keep him distracted.

"Physically, you're still a youngling. Erin would want you to be safe. She will skin me if anything happens to you."

The space to the right of the console bank shimmers like superheated air. Into that shimmer, a human youngling appears. Well, not quite human, he still has his tail and horns.

Avery gasps.

I frown as my son plants his tiny human fists on his hips, radiating anger.

"I did not agree to this," he says. "This is a violation of my intergalactic rights."

I blink a couple of times.

Lan chuckles. "I like him. He is both cute and highly

educated on his rights."

"We need to get Mommy," the small horned cherub states.

"We will," Avery says. "But you know Erin wouldn't be happy if you were to endanger yourself in the process."

"I'm not worried about myself," he says.

Before my eyes, he disappears and reappears again.

"With my invisibility, it will be hard for them to capture me unless they have infrared, which they might," he says like this is not a big fucking deal. "It is a risk I'm willing to take."

"Can you show us where she is?" I ask, because he's not fucking going, and I'm not sure how to say this yet so it doesn't piss him off.

He marches over to the console bank and jumps up onto the ledge, where the small engineers continue working. The green engineers move aside to make space for Brin.

My son frowns, as though familiarizing himself, before he starts tapping away.

"Impressive," Haden says. "Especially in one so young and with no knowledge of our systems. And he's exceptionally clever."

"He clearly doesn't get that from Kane," Lan says.

I whip the bastard with my tail.

"This is the place," Brin calls in his sweet, high voice that makes thinking of him as anything but a youngling a challenge. He points at a large austere structure on the monitor. There must be many floors and rooms in such a building.

"Finding her in there will be a challenge," I say, feeling despondence creep in.

"If you have a portable tracker," Brin says. "I can put Mommy's signature on it."

"There is one built into the helmets," Layton says. "It will show on the visor display."

"And how will you get in?" Brin asks. "Especially when you don't look like humans."

"Body reconfiguration," Layton explains.

"Oh," Brin says, looking impressed. "They will be very heavy if you put them into a small human body."

"Smallish," Layton says. "There is only so much we can do."

"Good," Brin says, nodding. "There was a man in charge of her capture. I've looked him up, and his name is Carlton. This is the ID number on his badge. I want you to kill him. He hurt Mommy and is in charge of the operation. He needs to die."

"Done," Lan and I say in unison.

The journey through the intergalactic wormhole is a far less pleasant one than the interdimensional portal we use during sleep. I feel like my body is being broken into a thousand pieces, which technically, it is. I am not ashamed to admit it freaks me the fuck out. The twisting, turning void of blackness, plus the sensation of being ripped apart and reassembled over and over again, is sure to feature in nightmares for years to come.

I land in a crouch, with solid ground beneath me. I'm in a long empty corridor, with white walls and sturdy metal doors leading off on either side.

It took time to prepare—more time than I would have wished. I'm also aware that time moves differently on each side of the void. The readout on my helmet visor display indicates that several days have passed for Erin, while mere hours have passed for us. An uneasy sickness roils in my gut, thinking about her being here for so long and what they might have done to her while trying to get information on our son.

To my left is a looming presence—a man is crouched beside me. I blink. I can tell by looking at him that it's Lan, but it's also not Lan as I have ever known before.

Rising, I glance behind me, checking for humans and my tail, but neither humans nor a tail is there. I understood there would be no tail, but it is still disconcerting. I feel ungainly without the balance it provides. My human hands, hidden behind gloves, seem small and inadequate compared to my own larger ones with claws. At my right hip is an automatic weapon, and to my left, a foot-long blade. I draw the automatic weapon, while Lan does the same.

"This is fucking weird," Lan says.

"Very," I agree.

The display on my helmet has a blinking red dot that's Erin, two floors up and to our east. "Let's go."

We make our way along the corridor for the stairwell access door our helmet display indicates is on the left. Brin provided us with excellent details on the Bureau of Extraterrestrial Control, or BEC, along with enough information on their uniforms to pass all but a close inspection.

Nobody is going to get a close look or the time to inspect us. While we may be only two, we are fierce fighters and former pirates who know how to kill.

We push through the metal door with a backlit *Exit* sign above. It's quiet in the stairwell, and we quickly ascend the two floors...only to stop, finding the door locked.

"I don't like this," Lan mutters, putting his shoulder to the door. It creaks but holds.

We don't have time for this. Waving him aside, I level my weapon on the door lock and shoot.

Lan jumps back as the lock disintegrates under the barrage of bullets. "What the actual fuck? We were supposed to keep it quiet!"

"The weapon is more effective than I realized," I say defensively.

Muttering a curse, he slams through the door.

A scream greets us. A woman throws a tray of glass vials in the air and plasters herself against the wall. I take in the angle, how our heads skin the ceiling. Either she is an exceptionally tiny human, or we are much taller than we should be.

"I think Layton fucked up the sizing," Lan says as a team of human males careen around the corner and come to a skittering stop. The woman runs toward them, screaming.

"Yes," I agree. "Layton is clearly an amateur at this space-time travel and has made us the wrong fucking size. Even had I not shot out the lock, we would not fucking pass for humans."

"Lower your weapons, alien scum!" a human male calls.

"Fucking great!" Lan mutters.

When we don't lower our weapons as requested, the first man shoots.

"This is ridiculous," I say, not putting my weapon down either because I'm wearing armor, and I'm sure Layton would not have fucked *that* up. Also, the humans are obviously trying to capture rather than harm us, since the bullets embed harmlessly into the floor and walls.

I nod to Lan, he nods back.

We charge.

The humans turn and flee.

No matter, we are faster. Turning weapons around, we smack them up the back of the head as they try to escape.

They go down, one by one, the occasional spatter of blood accompanying a particularly savage blow.

More humans in tactical gear spill out of a side door and promptly retreat when I turn my weapon the right way around and shoot. I slip one of the discarded human weapons over the door bar. It will hold them for a while.

An alarm blares in the ceiling, and a red light begins to flash.

CHAPTER EIGHTEEN

Erin

Pain and abuse have a signature that is difficult to forget. I have lived on Earth for almost five years, and before, I was with Mike and his purple-skinned pirate wannabes. During that time, I was not hurt once.

It was different on the street, where I copped a beating plenty of times. Sometimes, it was a single punch or a slap before I fought and got away. Then there were other times when I didn't escape, and I was beaten and left bleeding on the ground.

How slowly you forget, yet how quickly you remember

when it happens again. This is not only about the pain, but about the sense of helplessness.

They don't hurt me badly. Whoever the fuck this agency is, they want to question me. While I'm sure they have other ways of loosening my tongue, which they will get to soon enough, violence must hold a certain allure to people seeking information. Apart from the small slap back at my apartment, they don't touch my head, probably not wanting to impair my ability to answer them.

The rest of me is bruised and battered, particularly my ribs. A couple might be cracked, making breathing a challenge.

After an indeterminate number of hours, a doctor—at least he looks like a doctor, complete with a white coat—applies a scanner to my ribs and heals the worst of the pain. They want information on Brin, and the questions are relentless.

As if I would ever betray my son.

"Who is he? Where did he come from?"

"I don't know what you are talking about," I say.

More pain.

More questions.

Then comes the examinations. Doctors and physicians scan every inch of my body. It would be fair to assume they have verified I'm human in every way. Unfortunately, when they next return to the questions, it becomes clear they know Brin is not human. I keep telling them I don't know what they're talking about. I say it so often that I start to believe it myself. If I just keep repeating myself, perhaps they will go away.

They don't. They keep at me until my mind turns foggy. Hours blend into days, with only pain, healing, more pain, questions, and pain. There is no pattern to the abuse. I'm exhausted and sleep deprived, being roused in a myriad of hideous ways—water, discordant sounds, or just a simple slap.

The world narrows down to the next moment of abuse. I focus on breathing, the feeling of air flowing in and out of my lungs.

I'm thirsty all the time and start to hallucinate, to see Brin. Yet while they still question me about his whereabouts, they can't have him.

My son is clever, much more so than these animals. Perhaps he has gotten the transmitter working, escaped, or both. I'm so proud of him. It hardly seems possible that a street rat from Primus could have created something so perfect. My heart clings to hope, praying he can get a message through to his father and Lan. They saved me once, and I trust them to find a way to save Brin.

I'm swimming in and out of wakefulness when they come for me again. My legs won't function, not that it matters, since the two guards grab my arms and drag me along the corridor. The room they take me into brings a sense of dread. I have been in here before for an examination, although I can't recall the details anymore.

One doctor and two orderlies are already present when the two hulking guards drop me into a gynecologist's chair…the kind that comes with straps.

They hold me down and apply Velcro to my arms, thighs, and waist, and the fight is over. The doctor snaps on a pair of rubber gloves. The flimsy smock they gave me is pushed up to my waist. Even after all they have done, I still feel humiliated.

The door opens, and a sharp dressed man with dark-rimmed glasses enters. I've seen him a few times since the day he stormed into my home…and slapped me. Carlton is in charge of my questioning. Everything that happens to me is at his command. Groggy as I am, his presence still cranks up my fear.

An orderly wheels over a stand with a monitor and a curly lead attached to a medical scanner. It reminds me of the one the doctor used when I first arrived on Earth to check on Brin's development in the womb.

I swallow hard, fighting back the panic as the doctor splats jelly over my lower abdomen and presses the scanner against it. My heart thuds erratically in my chest. Could I be pregnant? Even if I'm not, they both came inside me, and their sperm might linger. I can't bear the thought of this doctor taking their seed from me…or my baby, if there is an embryo growing, as I now suspect there is.

I struggle weakly against the straps.

The doctor pauses and pins me with a cold stare. "I'll sedate you if I need to… Are you worried about something? Is there another alien brat growing in you?"

I'm nearly sick all over him. "I'm strapped down," I grit out between cracked lips. "I've been beaten, deprived of sleep, and questioned for days. Of course I'm fucking worried."

His smile is nasty as he directs the scanner back to my abdomen. I think about struggling, but I believe him when he says he will sedate me. No matter how much I might want to resist, it is far better if I remain conscious and learn whatever I can.

He stops abruptly and passes the scanner back and forth over the same spot before tapping a couple of buttons on the medical monitor, which is pointed away from me. Even so, I doubt my untutored mind would recognize the subtitles of a half alien embryo.

He calls an orderly over, and they speak in hushed whispers that crank my tension up another notch.

I'm so woozy, there's a risk I might pass out, and I stab my blunt nails into my palms to try to wake myself up.

Boom!

The chair and medical stand with equipment shake. I

think I'm hallucinating again until all eyes turn toward the door.

"Coms are out," one of the guards says, bringing another spike to my thumping heart.

"Stay here," Carlton says. "Let security deal with it."

The guards nod and draw weapons, training them on the door.

"What is the father?" Carlton demands, returning his focus to me. "We know he's not human."

My eyes start to roll back into my head. What's happening outside the room? Is it Brin? Please let it not be Brin.

Leaning over me, Carlton pinches my cheeks until the bones of my jaw start to crack. "There's something growing inside you, bitch, and it's not fucking human."

I've little leeway, but I slam my head forward as hard as I can within the bounds of my straps. My forehead connects with his nose, delivering a satisfying crack and his grunt of pain. I'm seeing stars, but I don't fucking care.

Blood splatters all over my gown as Carlton pinches the bridge of his nose, hand rising like he's about to strike me.

The alarm in the ceiling blares.

Pop! Pop! Pop!

Automatic weapon fire, and close.

Brrrrrrrr! Brrrrrrrr!

Carlton freezes, then nods toward the orderly, who snatches up the phone on the wall. "What the fuck is—"

The door flies open.

The orderly drops the phone.

Pop! Pop! Pop!

The doctor and the two guards drop like they were puppets and someone cut their strings. In the doorway are two of the largest humans I've ever seen. Am I hallucinating again? Too many days without sleep, plus the physical and mental abuse, leaves me unable to fully process what I'm seeing. Yet I sense the two men, whose proportions are freakishly off, are Kane and Lan.

Their eyes shift from me to the remaining occupants in the room. In perfect sync, the human Lan and Kane move.

Lan grasps the two orderlies by their throats and slams their heads together. The audible crack is shockingly loud. As he releases them, they collapse lifelessly to the floor.

A long sinuous tail snakes out from behind Kane. It rises like a cobra, springing a pointed tip, and stabs straight through Carlton's throat. He gurgles, then the tail, immensely strong, jerks him up before being yanked out in a sudden violent rush.

The master of my misery crumples on the floor, joining the guards.

"How the fuck did you do that?" the human Lan demands as he surges forward, not to open the Velcro fastening me to the chair, but to rip them clear out.

"I don't know," human Kane replies, lifting my limp body from the chair as Lan pulls the medical smock down over me. "I just wanted to kill the bastard quickly, and my tail was there."

"How did you get here?" I mumble.

"The same way we are going back," Lan says, just as a black spinning hole comes for me.

CHAPTER NINETEEN

Erin

"**Mommy!**"

After the oily blackness of the wormhole, my son's voice is the sweetest sound to my ears.

Safe. In that instant, I know my son is safe.

When I went into the wormhole, I was in Kane's arms. When it spits me back out, I have a vague feeling that I might be on my feet. Relief cuts them from under me, and I collapse to my knees as a small familiar body launches itself at me. Lifting weak arms, I draw Brin close.

My body throbs with pain, making touch almost unbearable, but the smaller form pressed against me, the familiar scent of his hair, makes any pain bearable. Brin hugs me tightly, his tiny tail curling around my waist like he never wants to let go. "Mommy!"

I hug him back.

Around me is the babble of voices and the rushing blur of motion as people move—not people, aliens.

At my sides, I sense my mates.

"We need to take her to medical," a distinctly female voice says, one I could swear has the ring of a human.

"Brin, you need to let her go," Kane says. "Mommy is injured, possibly drugged."

"I can't," Brin says, holding tighter.

"Fuck it, I'm just going to carry them both," Lan says before doing precisely that.

Soft suede makes a cushion for my cheek, while against my chest, tail still wrapped around me, is my son.

We leave the room of entry, heading along dark stone corridors. I close my eyes, letting the drone of voices wash over me, comforted to hear both Kane and Lan.

I remember the journey to Earth through the void being far gentler than this one, but on that occasion, I hadn't been tortured for days and deprived of sleep, food, and water.

"Where am I?" I mumble. Hearing a whooshing noise, I peel my eyes open to see a metallic door open.

I'm carried into a futuristic medical room. Unlike the terrifying experience on Earth, this one holds a robed Lamandas female who views me through concerned, dark eyes. Lamandas come in a variety of green shades. The doctor, I presume, is a pale iridescent color that reminds me of the Earth's seas.

"Let go now, Brin," Kane says, and the small bundle clutching me is removed.

Lan places me on a medical gurney.

"Don't let them hurt Mommy," Brin insists.

"Nobody is going to hurt Erin ever again," Lan says, a rough edge to his voice.

My hand settles over my tummy as everything that happened before Kane and Lan stormed into the room comes rushing back. I press fingers to my temple, feeling nauseous, trying to get the spinning sensation under control.

"My baby?" My words are the catalyst for silence as I blink against the stark light beaming down over me. "Please tell me if it's well?"

"Baby?" Kane says thickly.

"Allow me to check, my dear," the Lamandas female says smoothly, gliding over with a scanner in her hand.

"Are you with child?" Lan asks, his hand closing over

my other one, where it rests against the bed.

"Yes, they said I was…that I am." I blink slowly, taking in first Lan beside me and then Kane holding Brin's hand.

My chest softens with the simple joy of seeing Brin with his father—the Devlin male who is fierce and compelling, and Brin, the miniature humanoid version of him, with blond hair and blue eyes that are all me.

"May I scan you?" the Lamandas doctor asks, drawing my focus back to her.

The species is renowned for their high intelligence and trustworthy nature. They often take organizational roles in medical or business operations. You find them in most places over the galaxy, except the criminal underworld. I've never known any to be pirates or criminals of any kind. I glance between Lan, Brin, and Kane, who all nod.

"Please," I say to the doctor. "Is it okay? Would it harm them, going through space the way we did?"

"No, dear." She shakes her head. "There is no reason why it should, but let us thoroughly check, and then we can see about something for your pain and healing."

The scanner she uses is nothing like the basic ones they use on Earth. It resembles more of a slender pen, which she passes over my body from the top of my head down to my feet.

A green light flashes when she stops, and a report comes up on a wall monitor to her left. She scrolls through the information before turning back to me. "I'm delighted to inform you the embryo is in perfect health. Although only a few days old, it is developing swiftly. The system indicates regular monitoring is essential." Her face softens. "As for the rest of you…well, that is another matter."

Kane's growl is deep and full of murderous intent. I don't need to look down at myself to know my state. I can feel every bruise, every pained breath.

"I recommend the immersion tank," the Lamandas continues. "It is both safe and noninvasive. Given you are gestating a hybrid child, we can't be too careful. We have a few humans here on the base," she adds proudly. "I have extensive experience with your species."

"Okay," I say, a little nervous about this immersion tank but appreciating how it is safe for the baby.

"I'm going to be a father again," Kane announces.

"Maybe I'm going to be a father," Lan says, scowling.

"I fucked her first," Kane points out, tail swishing in a way that radiates menace.

The doctor narrows her eyes on both my mates. "Gentlemen, this is not the time."

"We are not gentlemen," Lan mutters as though deeply insulted.

"I think the immersion tank would be great," I say. "Only I've never used one before."

"It will be fine," Kane says, his fearsome face losing some of its darkness. "I've used it after injuries on occasion, and when battling for the mine."

"Battling? Where in the universe are we?" I ask, looking around the state-of-the-art room.

"Xars," Brin says, smiling. "You will like it here, Mommy. Kane is a mercenary, defending the mine. Haden said Lan could work here too, so we could all be together."

"Wait," I say weakly. "Haden…Xars… Like the books I read by Avery Sinclair?"

"Exactly," Brin says.

CHAPTER TWENTY

Erin

After a few hours in the immersion tank, I am allowed out of medical. Feeling better than I have in days, I am taken to a comfortable room, which I'm told belongs to Kane.

Lan busies himself making me something to eat in the food-bater.

Brin is talking a mile a minute and won't move an inch from my side. I eat a little food but I'm crashing fast, and I wake up in a huge Devlin-sized bed to find Brin tucked in an armchair beside me, a computer tablet in his hand.

"You're awake! How are you feeling? I'm going to send for medical!"

I smile. "I'm feeling fine, sweetie, better than I have been in a very long time." And I really mean it, I realize. I'm not just saying words, putting on a brave face for my son.

I'm thirsty, and he hops down to get me some water. Shortly after, the Lamandas doctor arrives, closely shadowed by Lan and Kane, to check me.

I'm doing well, just tired and healing. Even using an immersion tank to help, it still takes a little time. It's not only about my body, but the longer, more profound healing that takes place in your mind.

I meet the Ravager, Quinn, and his human mate, Harper.

I meet Haden, the commander in charge of the mining operation, and his human mate, Avery, the former writer of books.

I meet Layton, the Lamandas male who brought me back through the wormhole.

And I meet some of the miniature green engineers who work here, and whom I soon discover to be both industrious and playful.

I learn about Xars, the planet that is now my home, and about the Narwan who threaten the operation here.

And last, the most important part of my healing, I learn about the two aliens I have bonded to, and who are now my mates.

I wake up in warmth, cocooned between two bodies. The one before me feels like suede, while the one behind is covered in the softest fur.

A long sinuous tail has snaked between my thighs while I slept and wedged right up against my pussy. It moves gently from side to side, awakening all the glorious nerves to life.

My groan is cut off as a large hand closes over my lips.

"Hush, tiny pet," Kane rumbles against my ear, sliding his tail against my throbbing and very damp pussy with slightly more vigor. "We wouldn't want to wake up the wicked gargoyle in the bed, lest he decide he needs a turn, *again*."

My eyes flash to Lan's face a little above mine. His eyes are closed, and his breathing is deep and even. Last night was the first night they touched me intimately since my return. They had been waiting for a sign unbeknown to me that I was thoroughly well. They were gentle when they laid me down, yet there is a quickening in the air now that stirs a frisson of arousal.

The dark kind of arousal.

The kind that I have missed.

Fingers that can spring lethal claws are blunt and soft as

they skim over my side to capture my nipple, then Kane begins to tug.

"Maybe waking him is not such a bad idea?" Kane says, rocking his hips against my ass, rubbing his growing cocks against me *insistently*. Ahead is only one destination. I groan into his other hand, sinking into the pleasure. I am safe, and Brin is safe in a world where he can be free and flourish.

A sharp nip against my throat redirects my attention to the now—the plucking fingers, the thick, undulating tail, the sleeping gargoyle no more than a breath away. It wasn't the love story I might have written for myself, were Avery and I capable of such a thing, yet it *is* a love story and it belongs to me.

I come.

There is no thought to deny myself this simple joy. My breath stutters, and my body locks as the sweet rhythmic waves take me along for the ride.

The tail unwinds, leaving a trail of stickiness. One big hand grabs my thigh, pulling it up and open, before two thick cocks snag and sink a small way front and back. His other hand moves to my throat, holding, applying enough pressure to make me feel thoroughly controlled. His hips begin to rock, making nerves tingle as he works slowly deeper. Kane's tail winds around my thigh, taking over the task of holding me open as his fingers move to my clit, where he strums the sensitive bundle lightly.

My eyelids feel heavy. There is a wickedness about being pleasured by Kane while Lan sleeps only a small distance away. The bed begins to rock as Kane picks up the pace, snapping his hips against mine.

"What filthy sounds you make, pet," Kane says, lips against my ear. "Filthy, wet little human, taking her alien master's cock like you were designed for this and this alone."

I clench over his thrusting cock. The pleasure building in my ass is dark and delicious and counters the heady sensation of his back cock filling my pussy.

As is inevitable, Lan rouses and blinks before his compelling, stone face twists toward me. His heated gaze slides down my body, nostrils flaring as he takes in what Kane is doing.

"She needs to be taught a lesson," Kane says ominously.

There it is—the darkness I crave, the heated kind that makes my pussy pulse and my belly clench.

Lan rolls to his side, facing me, and cups one breast in his broad hand, squeezing it gently. "I don't think we can entirely blame her."

"Oh, I think we can," Kane says. "Had she stayed at Venturia, we would not have lost five long years apart. Instead, our naughty pet fled all the way to Earth, endangering not only herself, but our youngling...nearly getting herself killed in the process. I think we will need to remind her of her place. These humans are tricky. I did not heed your warning last time about discipline, and we must rectify that."

Lan rumbles his approval as my heart pounds with fierce arousal.

"Regular discipline," Lan agrees, skimming his hand down my belly, displacing Kane's where he was petting my clit. "She is close to coming. I think that would be a bad idea."

My pussy and ass clamp down over Kane's cocks, which are still, buried inside me, making everything throb.

I groan.

"You are right," Kane agrees.

He pulls out.

"God, no! Why?"

"It's true—humans are tricky," Lan says, smirking at my whining. "You have done a poor job of disciplining her, and that's why we are where we are."

Kane whips his tail around to lash Lan's leg.

"Ouch," Lan mutters, but he is grinning. As his eyes meet mine, I see a wicked glint in them. "This is a two-being job for certain, but I think we are on the right track now. How about Erin sits on my cock while you punish her pretty ass? She doesn't like coming around my cock. It's still a lot for her to take, and I think it would be a fitting punishment if you whip her while she rides me."

Kane growls, but he must agree because he snatches me up off the bed.

Lan rolls onto his back and fists his giant cock as Kane lowers me to my hands and knees, so my mouth is hovering over Lan's throbbing flesh.

I lick my lips and throw a glance over my shoulder.

"Oh god," I say weakly, knowing I'll be in for a rough ride yet so ready for this, I can hardly think straight.

"Indeed," Kane says. "We are your gods, and it is time for our little pet to worship her gods." He taps my ass with his palm. "Suck him off. Get him nice and hard. I want you gasping and straining when you take him into your hot cunt."

When I don't immediately comply, his tail whips my ass. It fucking stings, and I all but fall onto Lan's cock. Then I taste him, and I swear everything about them is as addictive to me as they claim I am to them. As I lick and lap lovingly at the head of Lan's cock, Kane backs up instructions on how to tend Lan with wicked whips to my ass.

"Good little pet, you can do better than that."

It stings, and it turns me on. I am between two sexy aliens, pussy wet and ready for whatever they will do. The punishment, the rising sting where Kane whips me, turns into fierce need. I want to belong to them, to be part of them, for them to claim me and never let me go.

Here, between my two lovers, my mates, I am finally safe.

With them, I can be myself, a little thief from a shantytown turned wannabe pirate, turned regular human, who was hunted by the government and finally escaped. Here on Xars, there is no judgment. There are even other human females I have met, and who, like me, have found a twisted kind of heaven in this frozen, warring hell.

Spank!

"Deeper," Kane commands.

I do my best to relax my jaw and accept Lan's thick cock. He rumbles his approval, cupping the back of my head and encouraging me to take more.

Spank!

"Is he hard for you, pet?"

I groan around Lan's cock. He really is.

Spank!

"Are you going to climb on his cock like a good pet? Are you going to ride him while I discipline your naughty human ass?"

Spank!

"Open your legs wider."

Spank! Spank! Spank!

I squeal around Lan's cock as the next few lashes land

on my exposed pussy.

"Don't come."

Spank!

"Fuck, she really likes that," Lan says approvingly. "Sit on my cock, Erin, right now. Or I'm going to fucking come, and we'll have to start this all over again."

I've never moved so fast in my life. My pussy burns and throbs where Kane whipped it, sending me into a frenzy. I'm oh so close. I clamber over Lan, my legs stretched lewdly around his thick waist. My hands look tiny as I grasp his fat cock, trying to wrestle it into position.

I groan, feeling sweat pop out across the surface of my skin.

Just to keep me focused, Kane whips my ass again. "What a sweet little pet, so eager for her masters' cocks," Kane says, tracing his tail lightly over my hip and thighs, making me shudder with arousal and tremble in anticipation of him whipping me again.

"Such a pretty pink ass," Kane says admiringly. "And she's so well disciplined. I believe our pet will be feeling this for days…as her hot cunt will be feeling all sore inside after she takes a good, deep pounding from your cock."

I snag the tip of Lan's cock and try to sink down, sobbing with frustration when I do no more than wedge the tip in.

Kane closes in behind me, one hand collaring my throat, the other gripping my hip, applying pressure. "Good pet, open up and take his cock."

"Fuck! That is so fucking obscene," Lan mutters thickly. "Watching her tiny little pussy strain to swallow my cock…" He grasps my ankles in his big hands and pulls them forward, then up.

"Oh my god!"

He lifts.

Kane's chuckle is dark and full of filthy intent.

I hang suspended between them, gravity working on me, tight muscles forced to give as I sink down onto Lan's cock. I have no control against the pulsing fullness. Every twitch I make only helps me sink farther down. Kane's tail whips against one breast, then the other, the stinging making me squeal and gasp…making me sink ever deeper onto Lan's cock.

Lan's eyes are locked on the place where we join, a darker brown stain spreading down his cheeks and over his chest. "Nearly all the way in. Fuck, I'm close." He begins to thrust up just as Kane tightens his hold, keeping me immobile as Lan starts to fuck me from below.

"Come for him, little pet," Kane says, teeth nipping at my throat. "Come all over his cock."

I shake my head. I don't want to…yet I also do. My pussy is full, throbbing, clenching, and my body is on fire.

Avenged

The fingers around my throat tighten, squeezing, bringing all my focus back to their control and mastery over me, just as a thick cock spears my throat. I suck.

I am theirs, a human pet, their mate.

I come, a dark, intense release that makes my body and mind soar. They come with me, spilling into me and over me, making me theirs as I claim them as mine.

EPILOGUE

Erin

For all Xars exists in a constant state of war with the insectoid Narwan, I feel like I have found a home for the first time in my life. Lan has taken a position as a mercenary defending the mining operation and works alongside Kane daily.

My mates asked me if I wanted to move somewhere else, both of them having built a nest egg of savings over the years since we last met, but I said no. Neither Lan nor Kane are the kind of males who would fit a regular job. They are designed for fighting, and at least here, they have a cause.

While I worry about them, it's tempered by my trust in them and their skills. All this aside, I have come to adore the little tiny green engineers who work here, and I love that they can do their jobs safely under my mates' watch.

Then there is my son, Brin, and how he has flourished in his new home, where he can be himself and show his tail without fear.

"I think it might have grown," Avery says, admiring Brin's tail as we meet for breakfast in the common room.

"It has!" Brin announces in his sweet, cherub voice that defies his adult mind. "And look." He swishes it from side to side before coiling it around a glass on the table, demonstrating his growing proficiency in tail control.

"That's amazing," Avery agrees, smiling indulgently.

He is happy here, just like I am. His active mind needs constant stimulation, and he's currently assisting Layton in the mining operations, where, according to the Lamandas male, he is making marked improvements.

As for me, I've got a job in engineering. I don't have many skills, having never been schooled, but I learned a lot from Mike and his crew about cleaning and refurbishing old parts. The work is satisfying, and I like to do my part and to contribute. Besides, the tiny green engineers are full of fun, and I spend most of my day laughing at their antics.

Then there is the baby growing inside me.

This one is all Lan's—a quarter gargoyle, according to

my Lamandas doctor…and a girl.

I can't wait to meet her.

Lan is glowing with pride that he bred me this time.

We make a strange and odd family, but that's how it goes in the great vast universe. I love everything about it, all the uniqueness of my mates, my child, and the future children to come.

If I could go back and meet the little broken street rat version of me scavenging for food in the shantytown around Primus, I would tell her to hold on and that better times will come.

The End.

BONUS

Erin

After a full day in engineering, I enjoy dinner together with Brin before going alone to bed.

This sometimes happens if there is either an attack or the threat of one. I'm restless, the bed feeling too large and empty without my mates. I drift into sleep, only to be woken by the rocking of our bed.

"I'm sorry we are late," Kane mumbles, snaking his tail around my waist as he presses a kiss to my forehead.

"We came as soon as we could," Lan says, pressing a kiss

to my nape.

I sigh, already feeling the slight tension leaving my body. I have suffered a lot of stress in my short life, and I still have nightmares sometimes, especially after what happened on Earth. When it was only myself that I was worried about, it was bad enough, but the threat to Brin and then the child growing in my womb, are infinitely worse.

"Please," I mumble against Kane's chest.

"Of course, pet," he says, helping me ease into place with my cheek against his soft, furry belly, his cocks bobbing in hopeful interest as I take them in hand. I slip one into my mouth and suck gently as I grasp the other and pump.

I wriggle closer, getting comfortable, sucking just the tip how I like.

My lips pop off, and I glance back over my shoulder, wondering what the holdup is.

Lan chuckles. Sometimes, he can be wicked for a sweet gargoyle.

"Don't be mean to our pet," Kane says. "You know she doesn't like to sleep alone. Give our mate your dick, for fuck's sake." He backs up this command by whipping Lan with his tail.

I snicker when Lan mutters a curse and go back to Kane's cock, wriggling my ass enticingly because I'm impatient to feel both my mates.

Lan groans and clamps his big hands around my hips to hold me still. "Do you need my cock, mate?" he rumbles, sliding his fat dick up and down against my ass.

I groan around Kane's primary cock, as he calls it, already drenched at the mere suggestion of him filling me how I need.

His thick fingers dip between my thighs, testing my readiness.

"Is she wet?" Kane asks, cupping the back of my head and playing with my hair.

"Our filthy little mate is drenched," Lan says. "She's going to need a lot of dick tonight. I can sense it."

I suck enthusiastically on Kane's cock as Lan finds my clit and traces circles around it.

"Breeding makes our pet needy," Kane agrees, scraping his claws gently over the back of my neck before gripping my short hair.

I moan. I'm so close to coming.

"I think she needs it rough," Lan says.

"Agreed," Kane replies. "A good, deep fucking in all her slick little holes to remind her that she is ours."

My breath stutters.

Lan snatches his fingers away.

I growl, about to set him to rights, when Kane's fingers

tighten. He forces me deeply onto his cock, just as Lan spears my pussy from behind. I fight the pull for one stretched, sweet moment, then I give in and let myself come.

"Such a naughty mate," Lan says affectionately as he takes my hips and fucks me from behind. My pussy has locked down on his cock, fluttering in blissful waves that make every thrust a tortured kind of pleasure. Kane keeps his fingers tight in my hair as he works me on and off his cock. They are both big and dominant as they use me without mercy, and I love every moment.

I can never get enough.

Lan makes that rumble in his chest, his strokes getting rougher as he chases his pleasure. I want him to come, to fill me. I clench with every stroke, determined to have his seed.

"Fuck," Lan mutters gruffly. "Fuck, that feels fucking good. I'm not going to fucking last."

"Open wider," Kane rumbles, grasping both cocks. He squeezes the heads into my mouth. It's a strain, as my jaw aches from just one, but I accept it because he wants me to and because I know he's about to come.

He does, and so does Lan. A hot flood bathes my womb, and another fills my mouth. Neither my pussy nor mouth can take the deluge, and I don't try. But I'm greedy for my mates' cum, and I suck and clench and take as much as possible.

There is cum on my chin, throat, and even a little in my hair. I love Kane's cum. It's like a special treat that doesn't diminish because I get it every day. The fat cock inside my pussy flexes, and more cum gushes out. It's hot and messy, but I love it, just as I love the sticky cock in my hand, and the other, I use as my personal soother. I lap at Kane's cock and give a last gentle suck before I give in to tiredness, knowing they will soon rouse me and fuck me all over again.

I used to dream of Earth when I was little, searching for scraps of food and dodging another beating, imagining it as a utopia where I could live free and safe.

As it turned out, Earth wasn't the wondrous place I hoped it would be. Instead, I found my heaven, my perfect home, here between my two fierce alien mates.

ABOUT THE AUTHOR

I love a happy ever after, although sometimes the journey to get there can be rough on my poor characters.

An unashamed fan of the alpha, the antihero, and the throwback in all his guises and wherever he may lurk.

I'm a new author, learning as I go and appreciate feedback of all kinds.

Drop me a message and let me know what you think.

Website: www.authorlvlane.com

Facebook Page: www.facebook.com/LVLaneAuthor/

Facebook group: www.facebook.com/groups/LVLane/

Goodreads: www.goodreads.com/LVLane

Amazon: www.amazon.com/author/lvlane

Printed in Great Britain
by Amazon